Lilian Jackson Braun

Author of *The Cat Who Had 60 Whiskers*

The Cat Who Dropped a Bombshell

NOW IN PAPERBACK!

"As comforting as a
warm cat in your lap
on a rainy day."
—*Booklist*

THE CRITICS ARE PURRING OVER THE CAT WHO SERIES!

"FANS WILL GO BANANAS."
—*Kirkus Reviews*

"BRAUN GIVES FANS WHAT THEY CRAVE."
—*Publishers Weekly*

"LIKE DROPPING IN ON OLD
AND VERY DEAR FRIENDS."
—*The Tampa Tribune-Times*

"BRAUN KEEPS BOTH PAWS
PLANTED ON THE SIDE OF CHARMING."
—*Los Angeles Times*

"DELIGHTFUL....[THE CATS] STEAL THE SHOW."
—*San Francisco Chronicle*

"ENJOYABLE."
—*People*

"COMPELLING."
—*Mystery News*

"BRAUN'S FANS DEVOUR THESE TALES
AND KEEP COMING BACK FOR MORE."
—*The Chattanooga Times*

"GLORIOUS CAPERS...
PURR-FECTLY
WONDERFUL!"
—*Inside Books*

"THOROUGHLY
DELIGHTFUL...SHEER
READING ENJOYMENT."
—*Detroit Free Press*

"THE MIX OF CRIME AND
CATS [IS] CATNIP TO
READERS WHO LIKE BOTH."
—*Chicago Sun-Times*

Read ALL the CAT WHO mysteries!

THE CAT WHO COULD READ BACKWARDS: Modern art is a mystery to many—but for Jim Qwilleran and Koko it turns into a mystery of another sort . . .

THE CAT WHO ATE DANISH MODERN: Qwill isn't thrilled about covering the interior design beat. Little does he know that a murderer has designs on a local woman featured in one of his stories . . .

THE CAT WHO TURNED ON AND OFF: Qwill and Koko are joined by Yum Yum as they try to solve a murder in an antique shop . . .

THE CAT WHO SAW RED: Qwill starts his diet—and a new gourmet column for the *Fluxion*. It isn't easy—but it's not as hard as solving a shocking murder case . . .

THE CAT WHO PLAYED BRAHMS: While fishing at a secluded cabin, Qwill hooks onto a murder mystery—and Koko gets hooked on classical music . . .

THE CAT WHO PLAYED POST OFFICE: Koko and Yum Yum turn into fat cats when Qwill inherits millions. But amid the caviar and champagne, Koko smells something fishy . . .

THE CAT WHO KNEW SHAKESPEARE: The local newspaper publisher has perished in an accident—or is it murder? That is the question . . .

THE CAT WHO SNIFFED GLUE: After a rich banker and his wife are killed, Koko develops an odd appetite for glue. To solve the murder, Qwill has to figure out why . . .

THE CAT WHO WENT UNDERGROUND: Qwill and the cats head for their Moose County cabin to relax—but when a handyman disappears, Koko must dig up some clues . . .

THE CAT WHO TALKED TO GHOSTS: Qwill and Koko try to solve a haunting mystery in a historic farmhouse . . .

continued . . .

THE CAT WHO SAW STARS: UFOs in Mooseville? When a backpacker disappears, Qwill investigates a rumored "abduction"—with the help of his own little aliens . . .

THE CAT WHO ROBBED A BANK: As the Highland Games approach, Qwill tries to make sense of Koko's sudden interest in photographs, pennies, and paper towels . . .

THE CAT WHO SMELLED A RAT: A drought plagues Moose County—and a bewildering murder case plagues Qwill and the cats . . .

THE CAT WHO WENT UP THE CREEK: While visiting Black Creek, Qwill and the cats must solve the murder of a drowned man before they're up the creek without a paddle . . .

THE CAT WHO BROUGHT DOWN THE HOUSE: Koko's stage debut is postponed when Qwill suspects the cat's costar may be guilty of murder . . .

THE CAT WHO TALKED TURKEY: A body's been found on Qwill's property, and now he and the cats will have to determine who committed this fowl deed . . .

THE CAT WHO WENT BANANAS: Koko finds a bunch of clues when an out-of-town actor dies mysteriously . . .

THE CAT WHO DROPPED A BOMBSHELL: As Pickax plans its big parade, Qwill and the cats cope with an approaching storm—and two suspicious deaths . . .

And don't miss . . .

THE CAT WHO HAD 14 TALES
A delightful collection of feline mystery fiction!

SHORT AND TALL TALES: LEGENDS OF MOOSE COUNTY
Legends, stories, and anecdotes from four hundred miles north of everywhere . . .

THE PRIVATE LIFE OF THE CAT WHO . . .
A charming collection of feline antics that provides an intimate look at the private lives of those extraordinary Siamese cats Koko and Yum Yum.

Titles by Lilian Jackson Braun

THE CAT WHO COULD READ BACKWARDS
THE CAT WHO ATE DANISH MODERN
THE CAT WHO TURNED ON AND OFF
THE CAT WHO SAW RED
THE CAT WHO PLAYED BRAHMS
THE CAT WHO PLAYED POST OFFICE
THE CAT WHO KNEW SHAKESPEARE
THE CAT WHO SNIFFED GLUE
THE CAT WHO WENT UNDERGROUND
THE CAT WHO TALKED TO GHOSTS
THE CAT WHO LIVED HIGH
THE CAT WHO KNEW A CARDINAL
THE CAT WHO MOVED A MOUNTAIN
THE CAT WHO WASN'T THERE
THE CAT WHO WENT INTO THE CLOSET
THE CAT WHO CAME TO BREAKFAST
THE CAT WHO BLEW THE WHISTLE
THE CAT WHO SAID CHEESE
THE CAT WHO TAILED A THIEF
THE CAT WHO SANG FOR THE BIRDS
THE CAT WHO SAW STARS
THE CAT WHO ROBBED A BANK
THE CAT WHO SMELLED A RAT
THE CAT WHO WENT UP THE CREEK
THE CAT WHO BROUGHT DOWN THE HOUSE
THE CAT WHO TALKED TURKEY
THE CAT WHO WENT BANANAS
THE CAT WHO DROPPED A BOMBSHELL

SHORT STORY COLLECTIONS:
THE CAT WHO HAD 14 TALES
SHORT & TALL TALES
THE PRIVATE LIFE OF THE CAT WHO . . .

LILIAN JACKSON BRAUN

THE CAT WHO DROPPED A BOMBSHELL

JOVE BOOKS, NEW YORK

THE BERKLEY PUBLISHING GROUP
Published by the Penguin Group
Penguin Group (USA) Inc.
375 Hudson Street, New York, New York 10014, USA
Penguin Group (Canada), 90 Eglinton Avenue East, Suite 700, Toronto, Ontario M4P 2Y3, Canada
(a division of Pearson Penguin Canada Inc.)
Penguin Books Ltd., 80 Strand, London WC2R 0RL, England
Penguin Group Ireland, 25 St. Stephen's Green, Dublin 2, Ireland (a division of Penguin Books Ltd.)
Penguin Group (Australia), 250 Camberwell Road, Camberwell, Victoria 3124, Australia
(a division of Pearson Australia Group Pty. Ltd.)
Penguin Books India Pvt. Ltd., 11 Community Centre, Panchsheel Park, New Delhi—110 017, India
Penguin Group (NZ), Cnr. Airborne and Rosedale Roads, Albany, Auckland 1310, New Zealand
(a division of Pearson New Zealand Ltd.)
Penguin Books (South Africa) (Pty.) Ltd., 24 Sturdee Avenue, Rosebank, Johannesburg 2196,
South Africa

Penguin Books Ltd., Registered Offices: 80 Strand, London WC2R 0RL, England

THE CAT WHO DROPPED A BOMBSHELL

A Jove Book / published by arrangement with the author

PRINTING HISTORY
G. P. Putnam's Sons hardcover edition / January 2006
Jove mass-market edition / January 2007

Copyright © 2006 by Lilian Jackson Braun.
Cover design by Andrea Ho.
Cover photo © Sophie Bassouls/Corbis.

ISBN: 978-0-515-14241-9

JOVE®
Jove Books are published by The Berkley Publishing Group,
a division of Penguin Group (USA) Inc.,
375 Hudson Street, New York, New York 10014.
JOVE is a registered trademark of Penguin Group (USA) Inc.
The "J" design is a trademark belonging to Penguin Group (USA) Inc.

PRINTED IN THE UNITED STATES OF AMERICA

10 9 8 7 6 5 4 3 2 1

Dedicated to Earl Bettinger,
The Husband Who . . .

ACKNOWLEDGMENTS

To Earl, my other half—for his husbandly love, encouragement, and help in a hundred ways.

To my research assistant, Shirley Bradley—for her expertise and enthusiasm.

To Becky Faircloth, my office assistant—who's always there when I need her.

To my editor, Natalee Rosenstein—for her faith in The Cat Who from the very beginning.

To my literary agent, Blanche C. Gregory, Inc.—for a lifetime of agreeable partnership.

To the real-life Kokos and Yum Yums—for their fifty years of inspiration.

THE CAT WHO DROPPED A BOMBSHELL

ONE

April was lovely that year! No blizzards. No hailstorms. No torrential rains with mud slides and power outages. Gentle nighttime showers irrigated the potato fields of Moose County and freshened the peony gardens of Pickax City, the county seat.

It boded well for the sesquicentennial celebration of Pickax City, 400 miles north of everywhere. Plans were being made for parades, special events, and family reunions. Jim Qwilleran, columnist for the local newspaper who had spent the winter in a condo, was planning to move his household (two Siamese cats) back to his summer quarters in order to be closer to the action.

One evening he was lounging with his feet up, reading and eating apples, and the phone rang with that sound of urgency that sometimes happens.

The anguished voice on the line was that of Hixie Rice, the promotion director of the newspaper and chairperson of the Sesquicentennial Committee.

"Qwill! This is Hixie! Is it too late to come over for a minute?"

"Too late for what?"

"I've got a big problem!"

"Come along. Refreshments?"

"Not this time, thanks."

Hixie Rice lived in a nearby condo, and Qwilleran had barely time to gather up bachelor clutter: newspapers, apple cores, and items of clothing.

The woman who rang the bell was looking harried.

He waved her to a sofa, and she flopped down, tossing her shoulder-length hair and kicking off her shoes.

"Do you mind? I'm exhausted."

"Are you sure you won't have a glass of Squunk water, Hixie?"

"You twisted my arm."

At that moment two Siamese cats walked into the conversational circle.

"Hello, you beautiful creatures!" Hixie cried. They struck poses to show off their sleek fawn-colored fur, their seal-brown points, and blue eyes. She said, "Koko has such a masterful, intelligent expression, and Yum Yum so sweet and appealing . . . Forgive me, Yum Yum, if I sound sexist." For answer, the lively female jumped into Hixie's lap as light as a feather, while the male sat tall like an Egyptian sculpture.

There was something therapeutic about Qwilleran's manner. He was a tall, well-built middle-aged man with hair graying at the temples and an oversized pepper-and-salt moustache, but the sympathetic look in his brooding eyes and his willingness to listen to problems attracted individuals looking for help.

"How's everything going downtown?" he asked.

In exasperation she said, "I've just had a frustrating four-hour meeting with the PR committee assigned to find a name for the celebration, and we got nowhere! Qwill, try saying 'Pickax Sesquicentennial' three times, fast. Try saying it once! It's a horrible mouthful, and hardly anyone knows that it means a century and a half. We polled the man on the street. One joker thought it was 'sexy-centennial.' We've been working on the problem for weeks, without any luck.

"The scruffy little town of Brrr celebrated their bicentennial with a 'Brrr 200' logo that was perfect for posters and T-shirts, and someone suggested 'Pickax 150' but we'd cancel the whole show rather than copy them! All they have in that town is a harbor, a soccer team, and the Hotel Booze! In Pickax, thanks to the K Fund, we have cultural, medical, and education facilities that—"

She stopped for breath, and at that moment Koko delivered an ear-splitting "Yow-w-w!" His bedtime snack was twenty minutes late!

"That's it!" Hixie cried. "That's the answer! The name of our celebration! *Pickax Now!* . . . Thank you, Koko! I'll see that you get full credit!"

"No! No!" Qwilleran protested. "Just say that the answer came to you in a dream."

The next day the name of the forthcoming celebration was flashed across the front page of the *Moose County Something*, with Hixie Rice crediting a member of her committee who wished to remain anonymous. Only to her friends did she admit that the name came to her in a dream.

Qwilleran first heard the "convenient myth" from his next-door neighbor. He and Wetherby Goode, the WPKX meteorologist, occupied adjoining condos in Indian Village, an upscale residential complex on the north edge of Pickax.

"Hey, Qwill! How'd you like the news! They've found a name for the celebration, and it's a terrific one. It's going to fire up local enthusiasm. Folks have been dragging their feet over the sesquicentennial thing. And do you know what? 'Pickax Now' came to Hixie in a dream, although she's hushing it up!"

"Is that so?" Qwilleran remarked.

"Yeah, she's one terrific gal! Well, I've got to go to the station and see if the piano's in tune. So long!"

Wetherby (real name: Joe Bunker) entertained his weather listeners by singing *"Stormy Weather,"* or *"Sunshine of Your Smile,"* or *"Blue Skies."*

There had been a reason why Pickax could not, or would not, emulate the clever slogan of Brrr's anniversary. It was a matter of pride, trivial though it might seem to outsiders. Pickax was bigger, but Brrr was older. The antagonism was felt even at soccer games, after which fans always rioted—that is, until the sheriff started attending with his dog.

It all started circa 1850 when the first settlers arrived in sailing ships and made camp on the shore of a natural harbor.

They called it Burr, a good Scottish name. When a sign painter made a mistake on an official sign, spelling it Brrr—since it was the coldest spot in the area—the residents, with good pioneer humor, decided to keep it.

Fifty years later, when the territory became a county, the town of Brrr expected to be the seat of government, but the founding fathers were obliged to look ahead and choose a central location for the county seat.

Now comes the romantic part. The government surveyors assigned to choose a site happened upon a rusty pickax wedged in a tree stump at a point where two trails crossed. And that is how the county seat became known as Pickax City. The historic artifact that inspired the name was now exhibited in the city council chamber.

But that was way back when. There were great accomplishments to celebrate in *Pickax Now!*

🐾 Qwilleran also heard the "handy myth" from Polly Duncan, the chief woman in his life. She lived in a condo three doors away, but they ended each day with an eleven P.M. tête-à-tête by phone.

She had recently exchanged a career as director of the public library for a new challenge as manager of a bookstore. Both jobs made one privy to the latest rumors, and Polly always passed them on to Qwilleran. He himself was not prone to gossip, but he had no compunctions about listening, especially if the scuttlebutt came from an impeccable source, such as Polly.

On this phone chat she said, "Everyone's delighted with the name of the celebration! It was said to be the result of a committee brainstorming, but there is a rumor that it came to Hixie Rice in a dream, and I tend to believe it. How about you, Qwill?"

Astutely he replied, "The important thing is *what* not *how*. The name puts an auspicious slant on the celebration."

"You're so right, dear. . . . What do you think I should wear to Mildred's dinner on Sunday? If the weather continues nice, she might serve on the deck."

"If she does or if she doesn't, I'd like to see you in your new blue pantsuit."

Blue enhanced the freshness of her complexion, the sparkle in her eyes, and the silvery glints in her well-coiffed hair, which may or may not be attributed to her belief in broccoli, leafy green salads, and a banana a day.

"Eat your broccoli," she would remind Qwilleran when they dined out.

"Are you taking anything to the party, Qwill?"

"A bottle of something . . . Pick you up at one?"

"I'll be ready. Come in and say hello to Brutus and Catta. Good night, dear. *À bientôt!*"

"*À bientôt!*"

Qwilleran was grateful that Polly had survived the stress of a major job transition and was her amiable self again.

The four neighbors who met to have Sunday dinner were comfortable friends. The hosts were Arch and Mildred Riker. He was editor in chief of the *Moose County Something*; she was food editor of the paper. The two men had been chums since kindergarten in Chicago. Their rapport was casual to say the least.

The weather was pleasant, and they had cocktails on the deck: sherry for the women; Squunk water with cranberry juice for Qwill; a martini for Arch.

Polly raised her glass in a toast. "Here's to the beautiful people!"

"Don't forget Arch!" said his old friend.

Huffing testily, Arch said, "We got a blistering

letter from one of your devoted readers complaining about your repeated use of the *C* word in your column. He's threatening to cancel his subscription."

"Let him cancel! I know him, and he's a cat hater. There are twelve million cats in Moose County, and I happen to live with two who are smarter than he is."

Mildred said, "Maybe you should set him straight, Qwill. Write him a strong letter. You're good at that!"

"Thanks for the vote of confidence, Mildred, but it's unsportsmanlike to engage in a battle of wits with anyone who is obviously unarmed."

"Bravo!" said Polly. "I hear we're going to have an heirloom auction as part of *Pickax Now*."

Mildred squealed with excitement, "And an arts and crafts show, and three parades. It's going to be so thrilling!"

Polly concurred. "And Hixie's name for the celebration is brilliant! The committee had been floundering around for months, and the name suddenly came to her in a dream!"

"That can happen," Qwilleran said quietly, suppressing a chuckle. "The way it's shaping up, I can expect a deluge of ideas for the 'Qwill Pen' column, and I won't have to go through trash barrels."

Arch jumped in. "How about writing three a week instead of the usual lazy two?"

"Only if I get a fifty percent raise."

The joke was, of course, that Qwilleran was the richest individual in the northeast central United States. His freak inheritance of the vast Klingenschoen fortune, based in Moose County, had brought him to the north country, and his disinterest in money had caused him to turn it over to a philanthropic foundation. The K Fund, as it was chummily called around town, had been responsible for most—if not all—of the improvements being celebrated during *Pickax Now*.

Polly said, "The problem will be to focus on the stimulating present without neglecting the nobility of the past."

That said they all nodded thoughtfully and went indoors for one of Mildred's delicious dinners. She was, after all, the food editor of the *Moose County Something*.

Mildred served watercress consommé, pot roast with an exotic sauce, and small potatoes steamed in their skins.

Polly said, "There's nothing to equal the flavor of Moose County potatoes!"

"We all know why," said Arch. "A potato farmer was using them to make hard liquor during Prohibition, and the revenue agents caught him and poured it all on the ground. . . . Pass the potatoes, Millie."

She said, "Do you know why we have so many potato growers in Moose County? They came from Ireland during the Great Potato Famine in the nineteenth century. There was a blight on the crop, and a million Irish died of starvation, disease, or drowning when they tried to escape in leaky boats owned by unscrupulous profiteers. . . . Sorry! Once a schoolteacher, always a schoolteacher."

The other three talked at once, protesting that it was all very informative.

"And how is Cool Koko?" Mildred asked.

"He has a new hobby. After a lifetime of making carbon copies, I finally broke down and bought a photocopier—a desktop model. Koko is fascinated.

He stares at it for hours waiting for it to light up or play music. If nothing happens, he extends a cautious paw and presses a button."

"Koko is so smart!" Mildred gushed.

"Or crazy," Qwilleran said.

Mildred said, "I hear there'll be several family reunions during the summer, and I thought I might run a series of features on the food preferences of each group—with recipes." She looked at Qwilleran speculatively. "Would the K Fund be interested in publishing a cookbook?"

"Absolutely! And I'll volunteer as official taster."

Polly reported that one of the staffers at the bookstore, a volunteer at the humane society, had proposed an auction of homeless cats rescued by the shelter.

Mildred clapped her hands in approval and said, "Wouldn't Qwill make a wonderful auctioneer?"

"Wipe that idea from your mind right here and now!" he growled.

But the two women exchanged nods and smiles, and Arch said with obvious glee, "Something tells me we haven't heard the last of this matter!"

"How's everything at The Pirate's Chest?" he asked Polly.

"Just fine! We have quite a number of book collectors in Pickax, and they think the name of the store alludes to shelves full of treasures."

"How nice!" Mildred said. "And how is the bibliocat doing?"

Polly said, "Many customers have never seen a marmalade before, and they swoon over his apricot-and-cream markings and emerald green eyes. That little cat charms everyone, but one day he hissed at a woman customer and bared his fangs. She was wearing too much cologne! She left in a huff without buying anything, and we had to turn on the ventilating system."

"How is Judd Amhurst doing as special-events manager, Polly?" Mildred asked.

"He may be a retired engineer from the Moose County Power Company, but what most people don't know is, he's been a lifelong bookworm, with an extensive library of his own. And his storytelling hour for young children is a big success. I think they like the grandfatherly look of his white hair."

Mildred said, "I know he's retired, but he seems too young to have such white hair."

Polly knew the answer. "It turned white overnight, following a horrendous experience on the job. He was captain of a crew of linemen working in the woods, looking for downed power lines during a major blackout. He narrowly escaped being killed by a falling tree. I think he took early retirement."

Arch said, "Those power outages always occur after a heavy rain. The ground is soaked, and shallow-rooted trees topple over like bowling pins. I wouldn't want a linesman's job."

Polly said, "He could write a book about his experiences—except that he's no writer."

"Qwill could ghostwrite it," Mildred said.

The other three looked at Qwilleran and he huffed into his moustache.

Mildred continued with her bubbling optimism, "I'm glad to say that Wetherby Goode has promised unusually good weather for our picnics and parades!"

The two veteran newsmen exchanged cynical glances.

After more conversation the amiable party broke up early.

Arch asked Qwilleran, "What's in your Tuesday column? Anything fit to print?"

Qwilleran said, "I don't give insider information. You'll have to wait and buy a paper."

TWO

Following the farewell dinner at the Rikers' condo, Qwilleran and his reluctant housemates moved back to the converted apple barn on the southeast edge of Pickax—close to the action, yet sheltered from the hubbub by patches of woods.

He was moving from the neighborliness of condo living to the solitude and privacy of a barn and acreage. The latter was one of the oddities of Pickax, a city full of oddities. This one could be explained.

Qwilleran's property dated back to pioneer days, when strip farms were the norm—half a mile long and no wider than today's city block. It had been the Trevelyan apple orchard, and the back road still bore their name, but a series of disasters caused the family to sell.

Once upon a time this had been a drive-through barn, where wagonloads of apples were unloaded and stored in a series of lofts.

When Qwilleran first inherited the property, there was a fieldstone mansion as well, facing Main Street. It became the theatre arts building. Behind it was a dense patch of woods that Qwilleran called the Marconi Forest. It was the habitat of a huge owl that hooted in Morse code. Next came the lofty apple barn—all fieldstone and weathered shingles for siding. The barn was octagonal with a roof leading to a cupola at the apex.

The blighted apple orchard had been reforested with evergreens and fruit trees that attracted butterflies and birds. And an art center stood at the site of the old Trevelyan farmhouse.

As for the barn, the interior was redesigned so dramatically that the few persons privileged to see it called it the Eighth Wonder of the World. To the owner and his two cats, it was Home. They lived quietly for the most part.

True, the interior space was estimated at four hundred thousand cubic feet. True, there were three balconies connected by ramps. But Qwilleran insisted that it functioned as an ordinary three-bedroom house.

The expansive ground floor was centered by a fireplace cube in stark white with three white smokestacks reaching to the roof. Around it was a series of open-plan rooms: a kitchen where Qwilleran fed the cats and warmed soup for himself, accompanied by a serving bar and snack bar . . . a formal dining room seldom used except as a conference table for official business and champagne parties for charitable causes . . . a roomy foyer where Qwilleran parked his two bicycles—a recumbent and a British Silverlight . . . a library where Qwilleran read to the cats as much as he did to himself . . . and a living room with two sinfully comfortable sofas angled around a large square coffee table.

All the dark wood surfaces had been bleached to

a honey color. Light came from odd-shaped windows cut in the barn walls.

The furnishings were exactly to Qwilleran's taste: contemporary, massive, comfortable. The entire environment suited the Siamese, who flew up and down the ramps, teetered across the rafters like tightrope walkers, and virtually disappeared in the deep cushions of the sofas.

When the three arrived home from the condo with their luggage the cats silently checked the entire premises, beginning with their water bowl and dinner plates (his and hers) under the kitchen table.

Their private apartment was still on the third balcony.

The wastebaskets were in their accustomed place, but empty. The crows were still viewable from the foyer. All was right with the world.

Qwilleran never expected or wanted to be the richest man in the northeast central United States, but he made the best of it. The philanthropic K Fund invested the money for the good of Moose County. "Mr. Q," as he was known, wrote his popular column, listened to what people said, gave thoughtful advice, pampered the Siamese.

. . .

"Glad to see you back in town," said the attorney G. Allen Barter, at the barn early Tuesday morning when he arrived to discuss K Fund business.

"Unusually mild spring this year," Qwilleran explained, "and a lot of excitement over the anniversary."

"Where are the cats?"

"Watching you from the top of the refrigerator. . . . Shall we repair to the conference room?"

There were two thumps as Koko and Yum Yum jumped down and followed the men to the dining area.

"How do you like the official name of the sesquicentennial, Bart?"

"Inspired! They say it came to Hixie Rice in a dream. Do you buy that, Qwill?"

"Of course! There are day dreams and night dreams, and the subconscious works both shifts. If I can't solve a problem by day, I assign my subconscious to it, and by morning I have the answer."

"Do you have this system patented?"

"I'd like to consider it but, meanwhile, the system—as you call it—has come up with an idea for *Pickax Now*. Once a week, for the duration of the celebration, the 'Qwill Pen' column will feature one of the 'late greats' of Moose County—deceased persons who left a memorable mark. It will be a thousand-word profile: Osmond Hasselrich, Dr. Halifax Goodwinter, Fanny Klingenschoen, simple souls like Eddington Smith. Even a scoundrel or two."

Bart said with enthusiasm, "The K Fund could publish a collection of the profiles. Do it, Qwill!"

There followed the dull business (for Qwilleran) of signing papers, making decisions, solving problems.

Then the attorney said, "Clients of mine have asked me to intercede for them in a request. Do you remember Mr. and Mrs. Ledfield, who paid three hundred dollars a ticket to attend a charity event here in the barn? Koko turned it into a fiasco that no one has forgotten."

"Don't remind me," Qwilleran said. "Ever since that debacle I've avoided opening this humble abode to sightseers."

"Don't worry. What the Ledfields are asking

won't bother Koko and might appeal to you. They have a nephew in California who is about to enter college as an architecture student. He says that the fame of this barn is known in architectural circles on the West Coast."

"Is that so?" Qwilleran remarked with a glimmer of interest.

"Their nephew would like permission to sketch the interior as part of his college entrance portfolio. As you know, many architects consider what you've done with the space to be an impossibility."

"I didn't do it. It was the work of a talented designer named Dennis Hough, who lacked the credentials to call himself an architect."

"You never told me, Qwill! Where is he now?"

"Where he'll qualify for the 'late greats' in the 'Qwill Pen' column . . . Okay, your clients' nephew can come and make sketches, as long as he gives full credit to the deceased designer. Incidentally, I've not seen any photographs that did justice to the interior. It will be interesting to know what draftsman's sketches can do with it."

Bart said, "On behalf of my clients, I thank you, and I'll see that you get a set of drawings.

"By the way, in case you want to see what the young man looks like, Mrs. Ledfield gave me a newspaper clipping with his picture, taken when he was a downhill ski racer. His major interest is skiing."

Qwilleran looked at the photo of an athletic-looking fellow dressed for snow, with a stocking cap pulled over shoulder-length hair. He said, "He'll have to cut his hair when he becomes an architect."

"Maybe yes, maybe no," Bart said. "Have you been to California lately?"

They discussed K Fund business while Koko sat on the table and watched closely. But when the attorney gathered up his papers to leave, the photo of Harvey Ledfield was missing. "His aunt wanted it returned," Bart said.

"It's probably mixed in with your papers," Qwilleran reassured him. He really thought otherwise! Koko had been hanging around with a mischievous glint in his eye!

After a lengthy career in journalism Qwilleran had his emotions under control when it came to personal events. He could be pleased, mildly moved, even enthusiastic, but never, never excited. After the attorney's visit he had to admit that he was excited about having the barn's interior sketched. He reminded himself that this young fellow was only a would-be student, not yet enrolled. And a draftsman's sketch was not the same as an artist's drawing. Still, he was too excited to wait until eleven P.M. to break the news to Polly in their nightly phone chat. He walked downtown.

With his oversize moustache and orange baseball cap he was recognized everywhere. "Hi, Mr. Q!" said pedestrians with faces wreathed in smiles. "How's Koko, Mr. Q?" To the men he gave a friendly salute; to women, a gracious bow, which would be described to family and friends. Qwilleran was not only the 'Qwill Pen' in person but the power behind the K Fund.

From the barnyard he walked through the evergreen woods, causing some flutterings of wings and scurrying in the underbrush, then across the parking lot of the theatre arts building and north on Main Street in the City of Stone, as the shopping center was nicknamed. Behind the post office was the new bookstore, The Pirate's Chest, where

Polly was enjoying her new career as manager.

He used his key to the side door, letting himself directly into the office. She was not there, but behind a folding screen Dundee, the bibliocat, could be heard scratching in his commode.

Soon Polly arrived. "Qwill! What a pleasant surprise! How does it feel to be able to walk downtown?"

"Invigorating! I'm really here to ask a question. . . . Do you know the Ledfields of Purple Point?"

"I know they're one of the 'fine old families'— very wealthy. Nathan is a collector. Doris was on my board of directors at the library—but not for long. She's rather frail. No children. Nathan's only brother and his wife were killed in a car accident out west not too long ago. Why do you ask?"

"The orphaned son, as I understand it, is coming here to visit his aunt and uncle and—you won't believe this—sketch the interior of my barn for a college-entrance portfolio."

"How very exciting," Polly said.

"Yes," Qwilleran said coolly, concealing his real feelings.

From Polly's office he went out to the selling floor, exchanged pleasantries with saleswomen in Green Smocks, told Dundee he was a good bibliocat and could expect a raise. He walked down the broad staircase to the community area with its view of meeting rooms, and the Edd Smith Place, where pre-owned books were donated and sold, with proceeds going to good causes.

In Moose County one simple fact encouraged the charitable impulses of the general public: The K Fund would match any donation dollar for dollar.

In the ESP, as the lower-level shop was known, Lisa Compton was the volunteer at the cash register. A retired academic, married to the school superintendent, she was the one Qwilleran wanted to see.

"Lisa, how would you like to collaborate on a 'Qwill Pen' project that will later be published in book form?"

When she heard about the "Late Greats," she was enthusiastic. She and her husband were third-generation natives. Together they could suggest candidates for the honor, and Lisa would do the research.

She would start with the late Osmond Hasselrich, pioneer lawyer, and Agatha Burns, well-loved teacher.

Back upstairs, he found Polly waiting for him with her eyes sparkling in a way that meant mischief or conspiracy.

"Sit down!" she ordered. "We have to discuss your birthday dinner! I've made a reservation at the Mackintosh Inn—your favorite table in front of the Scottish castle crest, and I thought it would be fun if we wore our Highland kit."

That meant the Mackintosh kilt for Qwilleran, with dinner jacket, sporran, and a dagger in his sock. Polly would wear a long white dress with Duncan plaid pinned on the shoulder with a cairngorm.

"They won't know it's your birthday. I'll tell them we're celebrating a moment in Scottish history, and they'll serve us two Scotch eggs as aperitifs, and you can have half of mine."

When assured that he would not have to blow out candles on a cake, Qwilleran agreed. Afterward, they would go home and listen to good music. He had a new John Field recording he wanted to play.

· · ·

Later that evening Qwilleran wrote in his private journal, explaining somewhat his panic about birthday celebrations.

Thursday—When Arch Riker and I were growing up in Chicago, he claims I was always a rotten kid on my birthday. He should know. He was there. And he was no sweet potato. Even at an early age, I recall, I despised the silly games played at birthday parties—and the blowing out of candles after making a wish—and the Happy Birthday song, sung out of tune and off key.

Now that I'm an adult, I find the same inanities are being practiced, and I have to smile and thank everyone when I'd rather break the cake platter over their skulls.

I know it's an eccentricity, and I have no intention of giving it up. We're all entitled to a few eccentricities, provided they don't harm anyone, break the law, or constitute a public nuisance.

THREE

🐾 One Sunday afternoon in late May Hixie Rice and a member of the Sesquicentennial Committee arrived at the barn to discuss various matters. Dwight Somers was a public relations counselor whose PR firm was called Somers & Beard, although the only beard was on his face. Qwill and his guests seated themselves in the sumptuous sofas and Hixie said, "These sofas are just too comfortable, Qwill! We may never want to leave."

"Don't worry," he said. "Koko has a built-in alarm clock and will throw you out. Talk fast."

Both cats were on the coffee table, huddled shoulder to shoulder on a very large paperback book. "What are they sitting on?" she asked.

"Their bedtime reading: *Mark Twain for Kids*." The cover had a full-length photo of the great author.

Hixie said, "He has a moustache like yours."

"Or, rather, I have a moustache like his."

Qwilleran was a great admirer of his predecessor's wit. It was Twain who gave the world's shortest advice: "When in doubt, tell the truth."

"Now, what's the latest about the celebration?"

"To make it brief," said Dwight, "three parades will define the thirteen weeks of celebration. On Memorial Day the theme will be *Pickax Past*, with historical tableaux on floats. The main feature will be the antique pickax that has been in a glass case at City Hall."

Dwight went on. "On July Fourth the theme will be *Pickax Now*, and on Labor Day, *Pickax Future*."

Hixie said, "I've been telling Dwight about the

one-man show you did, Qwill—on the Big Burning of 1869."

"How did it work?" Dwight asked.

Qwilleran explained. "We asked the audience to imagine that radio existed in 1869, and we brought them a broadcast covering the fire, which destroyed practically the whole county except the courthouse in Pickax. I played the radio announcer; Hixie was technical assistant, handling sound effects."

Hixie groaned. "Once we did the show in a church basement when the furnace was out of order. The audience was sitting wrapped in blankets and wearing earmuffs and mittens. And the radio announcer was saying that the temperature was a hundred degrees as he mopped his brow."

Qwilleran recalled another time when—at the most tragic moment in the show—a small girl walked across the stage looking for the restroom. "A few minutes later, she came back. It's to the audience's credit that they didn't laugh, but I had a hard time keeping a sober face."

Dwight asked, "Could you dig your script out of mothballs and do the show for *Pickax Now* audiences?"

Qwilleran said he believed so. Actually, he was fond of working before an audience, reading words that he had written, hearing the enthusiastic applause. "How many shows?"

Dwight thought one a week for thirteen weeks would be appropriate—and well attended. "What would you think about a Sunday matinee? In the opera house?"

"Better than church basements and school gyms, I say. Let's do it!"

The City of Pickax was ready for its great moment in history! Houses were painted; trees were pruned; street paving was repaired. Downtown, the sidewalk planters were a riot of pink, white, and red petunias, and cracked concrete sidewalks were repaved in the fashionable brick.

The stately old brick courthouse with its proud stretch of lawn was now flaunting its famous peony bushes.

By contrast, the Pickax City Hall had always been a civic embarrassment: a two-story gray brick building with a flat roof, small naked windows, and an unimpressive entrance door.

The police department upstairs was entered from the rear, and there was a jail in the basement. But this year Hixie Rice had made it a personal mission to beautify City Hall. The windows were given shutters; the two front steps were given an ornamental handrail; an important entrance door was coaxed out of an antique shop; and the windows, both upstairs and down, were equipped with window boxes.

Hixie accomplished all this with her strong sell, winning personality, long eyelashes, and refusal to take "no" for an answer.

Then the Downtown Beautiful Committee planted the window boxes with . . . pansies! Yellow pansies! The jokers in the coffee shops had a field day with the pansies and there were waggish letters to the editor. But the pansies flourished.

Three parades were announced with the first being on Memorial Day, with the theme *Pickax Then*. All signs pointed to good weather, according to the WPKX meteorologist.

Then Qwilleran received a troubling message:

"Qwill, I need to talk to you, but I don't want Gary to know. Don't return the call—Maxine."

She was the wife of the owner of the Hotel Booze in Brrr. They had been married only a short time. She had long owned and operated the Harborside Marina.

The message gave Qwilleran a sudden desire for one of the burgers for which the Hotel Booze was famous. Grabbing his car keys and orange baseball cap, he said goodbye to the Siamese, who followed him to the door. In leaving, it made no difference what he said. It might be a little Shakespeare in a sonorous voice, like "We few, we happy few, we band of brothers," or it might be "Hey diddle diddle, the cat and the fiddle" in a falsetto that made their ears twitch. To him it was never clear whether they were reluctant to see him go or glad to have the premises to themselves for feline shenanigans.

On his way to Brrr, Qwilleran reviewed what he knew about the town, founded two centuries ago because of its superb natural harbor. The hotel had been built on a cliff overlooking the bay. It had the proportions of a shoebox, and a sign running the length of the roof could be seen far out in the lake.

In large block letters it said: ROOMS FOOD BOOZE. No one knew the sign's date of origin, but it gave the hotel its nickname.

When Qwilleran first arrived in the north country, Gary Pratt had just inherited the hotel from his insolvent father but could not operate it because of too many code violations. The elder Pratt had been able to get by on the grandfather clause in the building code, but young Pratt needed to make extensive improvements—or else. Yet banks would not lend him the money because of youthful indiscretions.

Enter: Qwilleran. He saw something promising in Gary Pratt, and the K Fund backed the improvements.

Actually, the hotel retained its scruffy appearance, because that was preferred by boaters, fishermen, and vacationers looking for something different.

The Black Bear Café at the hotel was distinguished by the huge mounted beast rearing on hind legs, the comfortable shabbiness, the cracks in the mirror behind the bar, and the appetizing aroma of grilling bear burgers.

Qwilleran sat on the last stool at the end of the bar, knowing it was less apt to collapse and deposit him on the floor.

A lively waitress approached. "Hi, Mr. Q! Haven't seen you all winter. The boss is out shopping. Squunk water as usual? Burger medium rare with fries?"

Without Gary Pratt for chitchat Qwilleran soon finished his lunch and strolled down the hill to the Harborside Marina. Maxine came out of the office and led him down the pier that offered boats for sale. To all appearances she was selling him a cabin cruiser, but she was saying in hushed tones:

"It's like this: Gary was behind the bar last night and heard two customers making plans to steal the historic pickax before the parade! There's a certain element down here looks for ways to make trouble. When Gary told me about it last night, I said he should warn the Pickax authorities but he said it was unethical for a barkeeper to reveal his customers' conversations. Also bad for business. So I took it on myself to call you. Did I do right?"

"Certainly not wrong. Of course, there's always the possibility that a couple of drunks were indulging in bar-blab. Even so, it won't hurt to check the security at City Hall. I'll drop a flea in the correct ear."

Much relieved, she invited Qwilleran into the marina office for coffee, and they talked about forthcoming boat races and marine weather predictions.

That evening, Qwilleran phoned Andrew Brodie, Pickax police chief, at home—at an hour when a nightcap would be appropriate. "Andy, I happen to have some Gouda cheese—and what goes with it. Also a couple of hot tips. Put on your shoes and come on over."

A few minutes later, the big burly Scot burst through the kitchen door. The bottles were on the bar top; the cheese board was on the snack bar.

"Where's that smart cat? I've got a couple of investigations for him to do!"

Both cats were waiting with whiskers twitching in anticipation; Koko knew when he was being complimented, and Yum Yum knew when there was a good shoelace to untie.

The men sat at the snack bar and talked about

Pickax Now: the expected crowds, the number of family reunions, and the ambitious schedule of parades.

"And that's one of the reasons I called you, Andy," said Qwilleran. "It's well known that the famous pickax that started it all will be featured in the first parade on the Number One float—with blinking lights, banners, a drum tattoo, and a lineup of armed guards." (It was a bit of fabrication on Qwilleran's part, but intended to dramatize the situation.) "Now—get this, Andy—my spies around the county tell me there is a plot among an anti-Pickax element to steal the ax from the council chamber. Apparently they have an inside accomplice at City Hall!"

Brodie almost choked on a swig of Scotch. "Where'd you hear this?"

"I protect my sources."

The chief recovered. "Let them steal it! It's a fake! The real thing is in the bank vault!" Then, with hoots and guffaws he added, "I can see the newspaper headline: 'Crazies Steal Fake Pickax!' It'll make them look like fools!"

Qwilleran asked, "How long has the fake pickax been on display?"

"From way back. A collector on Purple Point offered the city the real one. He had a kind of local history museum. Stuffed animals and birds. Never saw it myself, but when I was in the sheriff's department, there was some talk about it."

"Do you know the name of the family involved?"

"Sure! Ledfields. Made their money in the mines."

Qwilleran said, "I often wondered why the pickax was not in a locked case. The sign even calls it the original pickax. I suppose it was the pioneer sense of humor at work. They always liked a good joke."

Brodie said, "I hope the rowdies don't retaliate with acts of vandalism. Ever hear of the teller that daubed profanity on the side wall of the city hall— and signed his name? That's no joke! He was from the town of Brrr!"

Qwilleran said, "How are they going to make the parade any different, any more spectacular than any similar event?"

"One thing I can tell you," Brodie said, "is

strictly under the table. One float is gonna honor the first inhabitants of Moose County."

"American Indians?"

"Nope."

"Prehistoric tribes?"

"Nope.

At this point in the conversation Koko started "looking at his wristwatch" as Qwilleran always described it. The cat would suddenly appear where and when least expected, drawing attention to himself in some unusual way. (It was after eleven o'clock.) Finally he hopped onto the bar top in full view of the snack bar and started giving himself a bath—a thorough bath!

"Down!" Qwilleran shouted, and he obeyed, but his ploy was effective.

Brodie drained his glass and stood up.

"Good grog! Good cheese! Gotta get home before m' wife calls the police."

Qwilleran floodlighted the barnyard and walked with him to his car. "Who's in charge of the parades? Do you know?"

"Gil MacMurchie. A Good Scot, he is."

That was all Qwilleran needed to know.

FOUR

Everyone liked Gil MacMurchie. The best way to make friends, he often said, is to be in the plumbing business, on twenty-four-hour call.

After retirement, and now widowed, he lived at the Ittibittiwassee Estates.

Qwilleran phoned him there one morning.

"Gil, I hear you're masterminding the Memorial Day parade. They couldn't have chosen a better brain. Is there anything the 'Qwill Pen' can do to help?"

"Sure would like to bounce some ideas off you, Qwill."

"Your place or mine?"

He knew Gil had never visited the barn, even for a plumbing emergency. "I happen to have some scones and marmalade."

"No contest! I'll be there in half an hour."

Qwilleran met him in the barnyard and calmly observed the amazement of a first-time visitor: first, seeing the lofty exterior; next the interior complexity of balconies and ramps; and then the friendly welcome from two Siamese cats, who had never met a plumber they didn't like.

Since the weather was agreeable, the men decided to have their coffee in the octagonal gazebo that was screened on all eight sides and close to nature. The guest had the honor of transporting Koko and Yum Yum in the canvas tote bag reserved for that purpose while Qwilleran carried the tray.

"Who did your plumbing?" Gil asked when they were settled down.

"The architectural designer, who was from St. Louis, brought technicians up from Down Below," said Qwilleran. "Neither he nor I knew the political correctness of using local talent. I've learned a lot since then."

"If you ask me, your 'Qwill Pen' has taught all of us a lot—in many fields."

Then Qwilleran asked a leading question. "I didn't know you were a parade planner, Gil. How long have you been keeping the dirty little secret?"

"Ach, mon! I never even marched in a parade. But Hixie said plumbers know everyone, and all I had to do was pick the right assistants. Smart lassie, that Hixie."

The assistants who were really planning the parade were: Thornton Haggis, county historian . . . Carol Lanspeak, drama director . . . Wally Todd-whistle, designer of sets and props for the theatre club's plays . . . and Misty Morghan, artist. They were all "idea people"—who had never worked on a parade but who were excited over the challenge, especially that of designing floats.

"They said the parade should be designed with a theme and a color scheme. The colors will be green and white—the high school colors. Every float will have the same style of banner running the length of it, one on each side. The floats will have catchy names, done in old-fashioned lettering. They said there should be sight gags and audio gags. And there should be an element of suspense."

"I like it already!" Qwilleran said.

"Yow!" said Koko, who had deserted the wildlife and was hanging around, probably looking for crumbs from the scones.

Gil looked at the cat warily and lowered his voice.

"I could tell you a few of the plans, but I wouldn't want it to go any further."

"Don't worry. Koko is absolutely trustworthy."

"Well! The parade is scheduled to start at eleven A.M. Five minutes before, a helicopter flies over the parade route streaming a banner: 'Pickax Then!' There are shills planted in the crowd all along the parade route to start the cheers and applause. Next there's a *boom* like a bombshell. There'll be instant silence in the crowd. Then another *boom*! And another. Followed by the shrieking sirens of police cars and the honking of other emergency vehicles."

Qwilleran said, "Eyes should be popping and mouths should be gaping by this time."

"Right. That's the audio gag. Next comes the

sight gag. Two street-sweeping vehicles appear. They're draped with green-and-white streamers, and the operators are wearing green coveralls and—*white tophats*! And they're sweeping the pavement. . . . Right after that comes the high school tumbling team in green-and-white tights, doing handsprings and back flips and generally jumping for joy. Then comes the first float."

Gil stopped to gulp coffee before continuing. "The first float has a banner—'How It All Began'—with the historic ax and tree stump on a platform—a cube about five feet high and covered with green grass. And it's surrounded by armed guards! Then there are drumbeats."

Qwilleran said, "I hope this is being filmed!"

"It's going to be televised."

"Yow!" said Koko, who had been ignored for too long.

Gil said, "I'll tell you about one more float, and then I've got to leave. The second float has a banner saying: 'They Were Here First.' It's a forest scene populated with a stuffed moose, elk, wolves, a great horned owl, and a bald eagle! All on loan from the Ledfield collection.

"Nathan Ledfield in Purple Point has a private museum in a big addition at the back of his house. His old man started it—or maybe his granddad. Anyhow, he'll leave the collection to the city when he goes if we promise to provide a building for it. . . . Is there any more coffee in the pot?"

Qwilleran poured.

Koko turned abruptly and showed a sudden interest in Gil's pocket.

A moment later there was an odd noise in the pocket, and he reached in for a cell phone. "MacMurchie here . . . Hmmm . . . Yes, he's here. I'll tell him. Sorry to hear it, but we knew it was coming. Thanks for calling." He slipped the phone back into his pocket and said to Qwilleran, "Well! Well! Well! . . . Homer Tibbitt died this morning. Too bad he won't see the parade."

"Well! What can I say? He was a great man," Qwilleran said.

This was the day Qwilleran shopped for Polly's groceries and stowed them in the trunk of her car in the bookstore parking lot. But all the while he was thinking about the county historian emeritus. He would be one of the "Late Greats": the anecdotes he had told about his early life, the papers he had written for the historical collection at the public library, and the tales everyone had to tell about "The Grand Old Man," as he was known. There would never be another. . . . No doubt Homer's "young bride" could relate a few incidents. Rhoda was eighty when they were married a decade ago; neither had been married before. Together they bantered in true Moose County style and amused their friends.

His weekly shopping for Polly entitled him to dinner at her condo—a pick-up meal, she called it, since she had been working all day.

Tonight, Polly mentioned, "You and I are invited to view the parade from the second-floor windows of the department store."

"I hope you accepted," he said. "And Sunday afternoon is the first performance of the Fire Show on the stage of the opera house. I'll see that you get tickets."

"Oh, I'm so thrilled! I've seen it twice, but that was how many years ago? Will Hixie be handling the sound effects?"

"Yes, if I can get her to come down to earth for a rehearsal." And then he said, "Do you know a woman in Kennebeck who does hand knitting? Bart was wearing one of her sweaters yesterday, and it looked pretty good."

"She sings in the choir at our church. Would you like one of her sweaters? What did you have in mind? It can be your birthday present."

He protested, but not strongly.

Polly went on. "She's fairly young. She went from bride to widow in a few hours. Her husband was a lineman with the power company, and on the first day after their honeymoon he was killed by a falling tree while he was looking for downed wires. The shock affected her mind somehow; she developed second sight; she can predict calamities—like hurricanes, lightning strikes, and so forth. The doctors at the state hospital are interested in her case. I'll make an appointment for you!"

During the dessert course (some apple tarts

baked by one of the bookstore's Green Smocks) Polly remembered the news from Purple Point:

"The Ledfields' nephew is coming for the Memorial Day weekend and bringing his fiancée! Doris and Nathan are delighted, having visions of the Ledfield name being continued."

"Did they mention the sketching of the barn?" Qwilleran asked, considering it of more importance than family bloodlines.

"Yes. The young man—I think his name is Harvey—said all he needs is an afternoon. Doris suggested Saturday afternoon, and I wanted her to call you and make the arrangements, but she's such a shrinking violet."

Qwilleran said, "I didn't know they had any of those on Purple Point."

Polly overlooked the pun. "She's a respector-of-persons and quite daunted by your connection with the K Fund and your 'Qwill Pen' column and your fierce moustache. Do you want to call her and confirm the date?"

"I wouldn't want to give the dear lady a heart attack," he said. "Why don't you call her and confirm it for Saturday afternoon? Then perhaps you and I could take the young couple to dinner at the Nutcracker Inn."

Polly said, "I think that's very gracious of you, Qwill."

"I'm only making sure I get a set of the sketches."

Then he brought up a subject that had long mystified him: Why do some persons live *on* Purple Point and others live *in* Purple Point?

The explanation: The long narrow peninsula extending into the lake was originally the location of shipyards where tall sailing ships were built, using 120-foot masts from the towering pine forests inland. When steamboats came in, the shipyards disappeared, and twentieth-century families built beach houses on the sandy peninsula. The occupants said they spent summers "*on* Purple Point." Around 1900, when fortunes were being made in mining and lumbering, wealthy families built mansions on the mainland within sight of the purplish haze that frequently shrouded the peninsula. They lived *in* the community of Purple Point.

Polly said, "There was—and still is—some class

distinction between living *in* and living *on*. The Ledfields live *in* the community of Purple Point. I've never seen their house, but I'm told it's magnificent. Doris invited me, but when I was working at the library I never had time to socialize with my board members. Having dinner with the dear ladies once a month was all I felt obliged to do."

"Interesting!" he said. "Do you have any more of these tarts?"

When Qwilleran returned to the barn, he was greeted by an exuberant demonstration designed to attract attention. Koko chased Yum Yum up the ramp and down again, after which he fought a battle with a scrap of newspaper. He clutched it, drooled over it, and tore it with his fangs—all in good fun, apparently. When Qwilleran finally retrieved the soggy wad of paper, it proved to be the missing photo of Harvey Ledfield.

"What's this all about, young man?" Qwilleran demanded. Koko never did anything without a motive. There was some reason why the cat took exception to the Ledfield heir.

. . .

Qwilleran lost no time in ordering his birthday present from the young widow in Kennebeck, as recorded in his private journal:

Saturday—Today I met the Kennebeck Knitter. Ordered a sweater—sleeveless. V-neck, tan with brown borders. My birthday gift from Polly, who also coached me.

Rule One—Call her Veronica. She doesn't like being called "Mrs." Does it bring back painful memories?

Rule Two—Don't mention her weather predictions. She thinks of them as an embarrassing disease.

For some reason I expected something spooky about the lady, but she's attractive, has a winning personality and a mellow speaking voice. Polly says she's a contralto. She reads the "Qwill Pen" and knows all about Koko and Yum Yum. Her cat is a gray tiger named Tiger. I gave her a yellow "Qwill Pen" pencil, and you'd think it was a gold-plated Parker pen.

She told me that her church is planning a fall concert with Uncle Louie MacLeod as director and she hopes Polly will bring me.

She also gave me some of the crunchy home-baked treats she makes for Tiger, but when I put them on the cats' plates under the kitchen table, they sniffed them and walked away. Twice I saw them return to inspect them, and the third time they gobbled them up! CATS!

FIVE

There was no such thing as business as usual in the days prior to the barn sketching. Pat O'Dell's cleaning crew scoured the interior top to bottom. Then Mrs. Fulgrove came in to dust, polish, and do what she called fluffing up—not forgetting to leave one of her unique notes:

"One of the kitties' dishes has a crack in it, which you should get a new one."

As for the two "Qwill Pen" columns, Qwilleran employed well-known tricks of the trade.

On Tuesday he would reprint *Cool Koko's Al-*

manac with bright catly sayings, such as "It's a wise cat that knows which ankle to rub" and "If at first you don't succeed howl louder."

On Friday he would reprint "by popular demand" witty letters from such readers as Dr. Bruce Abernethy, the pediatrician in Black Creek; Mavis Adams, attorney with HBB&A, and Bill Turmeric, Sawdust City schoolteacher.

Everyone loved these reprints—except Arch Riker, but his grousing was all an act, since everyone knew the K Fund owned the newspaper.

Next Qwilleran called his friend John Bushland. Bushy was a prize-winning photographer who had a portrait studio and darkroom in his home and also accepted freelance assignments from the newspaper and anyone else willing to pay. For Qwilleran he always forgot to send a bill. "I owe you one," he would say, referring to a hair-raising experience they had shared.

Phoning the photographer, the newsman said, "Bushy, I'm in the soup! Koko destroyed a photo I was supposed to return to someone in Purple Point. I won't go into details, but I'm taking a group to dinner at the Nutcracker Inn on Saturday night, and I wonder if you'd be there to photograph them. We'll arrive at seven o'clock."

"I have a shoot at eight o'clock, but I can squeeze it in. Any instructions?"

"I'm chiefly interested in a full-length portrait of the guest of honor—a tall young man with shoulder-length hair, unless he's had it cut lately. In any case, I'll be there to point him out. You can also shoot the group as a whole. I'll explain later. . . . And Bushy, send me a bill; I'll take it out of Koko's allowance."

On Saturday morning as Qwilleran groomed the Siamese, he said, "It's not every day we have guests from California, so be on your best behavior. If you mind your manners, you might be included in one of his sketches."

The cats were quite calm. As for Qwilleran, he appeared calm, but he was feeling more stage fright than he had felt since playing the lead in a high school production of *King Lear*.

A chauffeur-driven limousine brought the guests

to the barnyard. That was typical of the well-bred, well-heeled old-timers who lived *in* Purple Point.

The young couple who stepped out of the car gazed up at the barn with unabashed awe.

Qwilleran showed the chauffeur the exit circle. Then he shook hands with Harvey Ledfield—tall, young, and serious in mien, with a healthy crop of shoulder-length hair in the tawny color of an Irish Setter. The young woman, who said she was Clarissa Moore, extended a hand with a businesslike grip that belied her dimpled smile and curly blond hair. Qwilleran thought, Wait until Joe lays eyes on her. He'll light up like Times Square!

The cats were watching from the kitchen window, and Qwilleran explained to his guests, "This is the back door. The front door is in the rear. That's what happens when you convert a drive-through apple barn into something it was never intended to be."

They walked around to the rear (or front) on a flagstone path between weeds and wildflowers tended with loving care by Pat O'Dell's landscape crew.

Then they entered through the custom-made double doors—staring and speechless until Clarissa said, "It's so . . . overwhelming . . . I could cry!"

Qwilleran liked her immediately. He liked her even more when he discovered she was a journalism major in her fourth year.

Still speechless, Harvey wandered around carrying a camp stool, sketch pad, and pencil box. He was looking for vantage points for sketching. Clarissa asked, "Where are your cats, Mr. Qwilleran?"

"Call me Qwill. Koko and Yum Yum are overhead somewhere, giving you a security check. . . . Feel free to walk up the ramps to the roof, Harvey. The scene from every level is incredible."

"I can see that!" the young man said. "You two—just keep out of my way and let me think."

Qwilleran and Clarissa went to the gazebo with refreshments.

She said, "I'm sorry I didn't meet your cats. Aunt Doris showed me a scrapbook of your columns, and a lot of them were about Cool Koko."

"Do you have cats?" he asked.

"I have a British Shorthair named Jerome. He has won prizes. Do you know Brits? They have round heads, perky ears, and great golden eyes." She produced a snapshot from her shoulder bag.

"He has a look of nobility," Qwilleran said, "and I've never seen such lush fur on a Shorthair— or such a rich gray!"

"It's called blue," she corrected him.

"Interesting. Does Harvey like cats?"

"No. He's never known any. When I was growing up in Indiana, we had cats around all the time."

"There are excellent journalism schools in the Midwest; may I ask why you chose California?"

She flashed her dimples. "On a vacation out there, I discovered downhill skiing and it seemed like a good idea . . . but sometimes I get homesick." She waved her arm at the landscape. "It would be fun to work for a paper like the *Moose County Something.* . . . What's down this little lane?"

He said, "It leads to the back road. There's an art center down there, and they're having a craft show that you might enjoy. If you want to amble down and see the show, I'll go indoors and give Harvey some moral support."

Harvey was sitting quietly on the camp stool, looking up at the balconies and ramps and then down at his drawing pad. His concentration was too intense to interrupt but as Qwilleran watched, there was a blur of movement overhead and a cry of alarm. Harvey fell off his stool and a cat darted away up the ramp and out of sight.

Qwilleran rushed to the casualty on the floor. "What happened? Are you all right?"

"I'm okay. . . . Surprised, that's all . . . It was like a bombshell—but soft. Was it the cat?"

"I don't know. He's not vicious. Maybe he was playing games. He has a strange sense of humor."

Harvey stood up and shook himself. "I think I've done enough sketching."

Qwilleran thought, There was no blood, thank God. Koko's claws were sheathed. Did he think that tawny head of hair was on a dog?

"Go out to the gazebo and go down the lane. Clarissa has already gone down to the art center. They're having a craft show."

Harvey took his advice and they returned an hour later looking pleased. They had bought a fine turned-wood bowl as a hostess gift for Aunt Doris. And they had met an older man who told some fantastic stories about the apple orchard and the barn.

"We told him we were visiting you," Clarissa said, "and he said he knows you very well."

"Did he have white hair? That's Thornton Haggis, third-generation stonecutter, with a degree in art history. Since retiring he's taken up wood turning as a hobby."

"I think Pickax would be a wonderful place to live!" she said.

Harvey scowled at her, and Qwilleran quickly changed the subject, briefing them for the evening: They would meet Polly Duncan, who knew Aunt Doris. . . . They would visit the bookstore named after the pirate's chest buried on the site. . . . They would have dinner at the historic Nutcracker Inn, famous for its eccentric brickwork and black walnut interior.

No mention was made of a bibliocat at the bookstore or the resident feline at the inn.

. . .

When they picked up Polly at The Pirate's Chest, Clarissa was quick to notice the bronze sculpture of a cat on a pedestal in the park. Harvey was shown the pirate's chest excavated on the site of the new building. Then Clarissa staged a maudlin scene with Dundee. Later, driving to the inn, the two women charmed each other with girl talk in the backseat, and Qwilleran entertained the guest of honor with a capsule account of Moose County's two-century history.

At the Nutcracker Inn there was time to walk down to the creek where ducks and ducklings performed their well-rehearsed ballet in return for morsels of bread that the host happened to have in his pocket.

In the lobby of the inn they were met by a sleek black cat named Nicodemus—and the photographer.

With hints from the host, Bushy snapped full-length portraits of the guest of honor, while Clarissa gushed over Nicodemus. Then Wetherby Goode appeared, and Qwilleran requested a group shot of the four guests. Before anyone knew what was happening, the photographer was dismissed with a wink and the group went in to dinner.

At the table it took Clarissa and the weatherman all of sixty seconds to discover they were ailurophiles. He said his Jet Stream knew more about an approaching storm than the meteorologists did. She said her Jerome had won first prize in a cat fashion show, costumed as Santa Claus. Polly related how her Siamese had a personality problem until she changed its name from Bootsie to Brutus. Qwilleran told how Koko had found a missing person buried in a sand dune.

Then Harvey told, solemnly, about Koko's aerial attack, and the other three guests found it hilariously funny. And when Wetherby quipped about "raining cats and dogs" the two women were convulsed with laughter again.

Harvey was not amused. Qwilleran gave a signal, and the weatherman went to the piano and played "Kitten on the Keys" very fast.

Later, during dinner, Clarissa said, "I saw a distinguished-looking man with a guide dog downtown. Who is he?"

The three locals talked all at once:

"Burgess Campbell, blind from birth."

"Comes from a very old family."

"His dog is Alexander."

"He lectures on American history at the community college."

"Burgess, not the dog," said Wetherby.

After a few smirks they went on.

"He instills his students with a sense of creative community involvement," Qwilleran added.

"He sounds wonderful. Wish I could interview him for my school paper."

"We're leaving early Monday morning," Harvey snapped.

To change the mood Polly said, "Tell them about the Civilian Fire Watch, Qwill."

He nodded sagely. "First you have to understand that two hundred square miles of this county were destroyed by forest fire in 1869. Ever since, the population has dreaded wildfires in the dry season. Burgess's students organized a round-the-clock patrol of country roads by volunteers working in four-hour shifts and reporting by cell phone. Everyone cooperated enthusiastically."

Wetherby said, "Tell them about your historical show on the Great Fire."

"It will run for thirteen Sunday matinees, starting tomorrow; and I can get you two tickets if you're interested."

Harvey said, "I'm afraid we have to spend Sunday with my aunt and uncle."

"Too bad," Wetherby said. "Perhaps you'll be back before the summer's over." He eyed Clarissa invitingly.

After the other three had left for Purple Point, Qwilleran and Polly drove to Pickax.

He said, "You and Clarissa seemed to spend a long time in the ladies' room, if you'll pardon an indelicate observation."

"She wanted to talk," Polly said. "It amused her that she and Harvey were given separate rooms *at opposite ends of a very long hall*. Then Doris was shocked that Harvey had not given her an engagement ring. He said he couldn't afford one, so Doris gave him one of her diamonds to put on Clarissa's finger in a solemn ceremony—which Harvey thought was silly. Clarissa was deeply touched."

"Hmmm" was Qwilleran's only comment.

He said, "Is it too late to stop at the barn for a Mahler symphony?"

Polly thought it would be an appropriate finale to a most interesting evening. And after all, it was Saturday night.

The day following the barn sketching, Koko was still not himself. Now Qwilleran knew the origin of the expression "Nervous as a cat." "Cool Koko," as he was known, was anything but cool, leading Qwilleran to write the following in his private journal:

Sunday—Why is Koko acting so unusual? Is he trying to tell me something? In all the years we have lived in the barn, he has never dropped from a balcony onto an innocent bystander! Perhaps Harvey isn't so innocent. That raises a challenging question!

Harvey and his fiancée were still in town today, spending time with the aunt and uncle. I'd be curious to know what that entails.

One thing I know for certain: Koko's aerial assault was not a mere whim. Nor did the color of the man's hair tantalize the cat. It's something deeper than that.

The guy's an ailurophobe, but that's nothing new, and I do believe that Koko considers them more to be pitied than scorned.

SIX

On Memorial Day, Qwilleran and Polly appeared in the women's lingerie department on the second floor of the Lanspeak store. Large windows overlooked the parade route, and there were folding chairs borrowed from Dingleberry's Funeral Home as well as some tall bar stools lent by Harry's Pub . . . not to mention a few plaster mannequins in chiffon nightgowns, lace-trimmed slips, and black satin teddies.

Others who had been invited were Hixie Rice

and Dwight Somers, Gil MacMurchie, and certain community leaders.

The Ledfields had been invited because they had lent historic objects for the float, but said they were suffering from allergies; June was the month for sniffing and sneezing in Moose County.

The audio gags were effective. The sight gags were beguiling. Then came the floats depicting *Pickax Then*:

HOW IT ALL STARTED . . . The famous pickax.

THEY WERE HERE FIRST . . . Wildlife—fine examples of the taxidermist's art.

BE IT EVER SO HUMBLE . . . The interior of a pioneer cabin with fire glowing on the hearth, a cook pot on a tripod, mother rocking a cradle, small boy reading a large picture book, older sister sewing, father arriving home with shotgun and a brace of rabbits.

DEAR OLD GOLDEN SCHOOLDAYS . . . Children sitting on wooden benches, schoolmarm, looking stern and rapping a ruler on a table piled with old books.

LONG BEFORE SUPERMARKETS . . . A barnyard scene with live cow and farmer with milk pail, chickens in coops, children carrying egg baskets, a sack of corn.

SUNDAY GO-TO-MEETIN'...Family dressed in their Sunday best, sitting on backless benches, hymnbooks open, preacher pounding the pulpit, choir of three primly dressed singers.

THE OLD VILLAGE STORE ... Clerk measuring calico for a customer, small boy ogling candy jars, loafers playing checkers on the old cracker barrel.

WITH THIS RING I THEE WED . . . Bride and groom sitting for photographer, box camera on a tripod and his head under a black cloth, attendants throwing confetti at spectators on the sidewalk.

The parade ended with a laugh: a marching band of clodhoppers wearing raggle-taggle garb, plodding along, hopelessly out of step, playing "*Yankee Doodle Dandy*" and hitting wrong notes with joyful abandon. They were the high school band—having fun, acting up, burlesquing the Good Old Days.

The crowd on the sidelines went wild with cheers and whistles, and the distinguished onlookers in the second-floor window laughed and applauded and congratulated Gil MacMurchie for a job well done.

Qwilleran said, "All the performers on the floats were members of the theatre club and had Carol and Larry for directors. It shows!"

"I appreciate watching a parade from a comfortable chair—behind glass—but I wonder if we missed some of the sound effects: the farmer playing his harmonica to his cow, for example." Polly said, "And the three choir singers in the Sunday-meeting scene told me they were going to sing hymns in three-part harmony."

Qwilleran scribbled a limerick on an index card—anonymously—and slipped it to Hixie:

Old folks all remember how
Every family had a cow.
Life was slow
And prices were low,
But I'd rather live in Pickax now.

After the parade, Qwilleran and Polly went to the barn for some classical music. Polly had wanted to pack a picnic lunch, but he knew what it would comprise, and he insisted on ordering from the caterer. When they arrived at the barn, Celia Robinson had delivered roast beef and cheddar sandwiches on rye, avocado and papaya salad, and lemon bars.

Polly was politely enthusiastic over the picnic fare; Qwilleran felt she really preferred that other stuff, but he pretended to be pleased that she was pleased. To take her mind off the calories he said, "I overheard spectators at the parade talking about 'Shooting and Poisoning.' Is that some lurid TV special that I'm missing?" (At the barn, the only TV was in the cats' quarters, and they watched only wildlife features.)

Polly explained that they were talking about the Kennebeck woman who has second sight and had predicted shooting and poisoning during *Pickax Now*. This was the first time that she had predicted a crime—man against man.

"The poisoning I can understand," he said. "All those family reunions, all those picnics, all that potato salad."

"Oh, Qwill . . ." she chided and changed the subject.

. . .

The day after the parade, it was back to work for Qwilleran.

The families scheduling reunions in Pickax during the summer may have suggested ideas for his twice-weekly column, but his real interest was pure curiosity: He had never been a member of a family.

In Chicago he grew up with only a mother, his father having died before he was born. No brothers or sisters, no grandparents, no aunts and uncles. Arch Riker was his best friend, and Mr. Riker did fatherly service for both boys: advice, sandlot baseball, trips to the zoo. Even now, the only members of Qwilleran's "family" were two Siamese cats.

In Pickax the host families of reunions were exhorted to register their plans and receive help with accommodations, entertainment reservations, and restaurant availabilities.

Qwilleran went downtown to ask some questions and picked up a copy of the newspaper in the dispenser outside the store. Across the bottom of the front page was a two-line heading:

THE LAUGH'S ON YOU, FELLAS!
YOU STOLE A FAKE PICKAX!

The police chief had been right: Maxine Pratt had been right. Qwilleran shrugged it off and went to the desk in the store lobby, where Thornton Haggis was on duty as registrar, asking, "Do you accept registrations for families of three?"

Without missing a beat Thorn asked, "Are they interested in sports, plays, music, art shows, antiques? How about a dog show? How about a cat fashion show?"

"What! Are we having one of those abominations here?" Qwilleran's shock was genuine.

"They say they're very popular all over—with cat clubs, pet owners, and the general public. You're dragging your feet, Qwill!"

"Let's change the subject, Thorn, before I burst a blood vessel."

"Well . . . I'm organizing a tour of old cemeteries that might interest you: forgotten graveyards, old tombstones, a few raunchy inscriptions. I have them all catalogued, and the old account books of Haggis Monument Works can tell visitors how much their ancestors paid for their grave markers. At one time in history, five dollars was a lot to pay for a tombstone."

"One question, Thorn. What is it that draws so many relatives together—from such great distances? It must be an emotion I've never felt."

"I daresay. It all boils down to family feeling, a consuming interest in your own flesh and blood— their successes, exploits, travels, even setbacks—a chance to see how the kids have grown, who has dyed her hair, who is gaining weight. It seems to be a middle-class phenomenon."

"How many families have signed up, Thorn? Could I spend a morning or afternoon with one group—just to see what they do, what they talk about, what they eat, how far they've traveled to be part of *Pickax Now*?"

"Take your pick!" said the registrar. "Any one of them would think it an honor. Here's the list."

There were names he had never heard before, and names that were too well known, but "Ogilvie-Fugtree" sounded inviting. He had known Mitch Ogilvie when the young bachelor was managing the Farmhouse Museum and later when he married a descendant of Captain Fugtree. She was a goat farmer, and Mitch was learning to make cheese. They lived in the captain's historic farmhouse—a tall, stately, Victorian mansion.

Actually, Qwilleran knew more about the couple than he could use in a column, but he felt comfortable with them.

"Sign me up for a Saturday afternoon visit, Thorn," he said. "And by the way, I sent a young couple down to the art center Saturday, and they bought one of your bowls for a gift. I hear you mesmerized them with some of your tall tales."

"I don't know about that, but they said they were visiting the Ledfields in Purple Point, so I completed their education."

One morning Qwilleran said to the attentive Siamese, "Your uncle George is coming again. Do your ablutions before he gets here, and don't forget to wash behind your ears."

"Uncle George" was G. Allen Barter, the attorney. To Qwilleran he was "Bart"—more of a pun than most persons realized.

When Bart arrived, the four trooped into the dining room, single file, ready for business.

The attorney said, "I searched my briefcase backwards and forward for that news photo of Harvey Ledfield. So did my wife, who has an eagle eye. Today is her birthday, by the way, and I'm taking her to dinner at the Boulder House Inn—just the two of us."

From a pencil holder Qwilleran plucked a fat yellow lead pencil stamped "Qwill Pen" in gold. "Give her this—with my birthday wishes, Bart."

"She'll be ecstatic! She's won three pens in your reader competitions, and she displays them like silver trophies."

Qwilleran said, "You married a Gemini, you lucky dog! That means she's not only eagle-eyed but strong, kind, talented, smart, physically attractive—"

"How do you know all this esoteric guff?"

With a feigned show of modesty Qwilleran said, "I happen to be a Gemini myself."

"I should have suspected one of your sly tricks! . . . What are those photos?" He pointed toward two eight-by-ten glossies.

"Oh, those!" Qwilleran said casually. "When I took my guests to dinner at the Nutcracker Inn on Saturday night, there happened to be a news photographer in the lobby, and he made shots of my party and the guest of honor, solo. You might like to give them to Harvey's aunt to replace the missing news clipping."

"Very kind of you, Qwill. And how did the sketching go?"

"He seemed to be impressed. His fiancée is charming. They walked down the lane to the art center and bought a turned-wood bowl for Harvey's aunt. It's a work of art—but a far cry from the silver-and-porcelain bowls she probably has in her collection."

With an abrupt change of mood the attorney said, "I had a call from one of their secretaries this morning, canceling their appointment. Both Mr. and Mrs. Ledfield are 'indisposed.' Allergy symptoms."

"How many secretaries do they have?" Qwilleran interrupted.

"One to handle their financial undertakings, which are extensive, and one to handle their collectibles."

Qwilleran said, "I hope their condition is nothing serious."

"My wife calls this area Pollen Paradise. Every second person you meet has a red nose, red eyes, and a box of tissues. One would think the Ledfields, having lived here for three generations, would know how to deal with pollen."

Qwilleran thought, There were questions that could be asked, but attorneys don't talk about their clients, especially to a newspaperman.

Uncle George changed the subject. "How did the cats react to having an architectural draftsman in their private domain?"

"Yum Yum stayed out of sight, but Koko surprised us all with his interest in the operation. . . . And, by the way, Bart, someone was telling me that the Ledfields are bequeathing their historical collections to Moose County for the establishment of a museum—provided the county erects a suitable building. Is that a fact?"

"It's in the will, but I don't see it happening in the foreseeable future. The Ledfields appear to be long-lived. Nathan's father lived to be eighty and his grandfather ninety."

"But that was before freeway fatalities, plane crashes, and deranged snipers," Qwilleran said. "Not to mention [he added whimsically] a new strain of hay fever imported from Outer Space."

"Yow!" Koko interrupted petulantly. His noontime snack was behind schedule.

"Meeting adjourned," the attorney said as he stuffed papers into his briefcase.

SEVEN

On Friday morning, as Qwilleran was preparing their breakfast, the cats huddled on top of the bar, waiting for the sideshow. They liked to be entertained, and he liked an audience. On this occasion he recited from his collection of limericks:

I live with a pair of Siamese
Who think they can do whatever they please.
They subsist on steak
And truffles and cake
And lobster and six kinds of cheese.

Two furry bodies bolted from the bar top and chased each other up and down the ramp—twice. There was something about the rhyme and rhythm of limericks and other homely verses that pricked their psyche and teed off a mad race.

Returning to the kitchen with appetites whetted, they polished off two plates of turkey scraps from Lois's Luncheonette. As he watched them enjoying their meal, the phone rang.

Koko's ear twitching told him it was friend, not foe.

"Good morning!" he answered in the unctuously musical voice that amused his close associates.

"Qwill! I've just received a very . . . interesting letter!" It was Polly's voice, brimming with excitement.

"About what?" he asked.

"Wait until you read it!"

"Would it be too presumptuous to ask who sent it?"

"Clarissa Moore!"

"Hmmm . . . Read it to me."

"It's too long and too personal."

"Then we'll go to dinner tonight, and you can bring it with you," he suggested.

"Tonight is my Bird Club meeting. Why don't you come over to the bookstore for a few minutes. You can park your bicycle in the office."

He agreed, wondering what Harvey Ledfield's fiancée could be writing about: Jerome? Invitation to a wedding?

"I'll be there as soon as I brush the cats. Want me to pick up something for your lunch?"

"Thanks, dear, but I've brought my lunch."

He had guessed as much and he knew what it would be!

Qwilleran finished brushing the cats and told them he was going to visit Dundee and read a letter from Jerome's mother. Then he added, "Let's hope the Ledfield heir isn't suing you, Koko, for an unprovoked attack!"

Qwilleran had planned to bike to the newspaper office to file copy for his Friday column, but his built-in itch to know the latest news caused him to detour to the bookstore. He was pedaling his British Silverlight that stopped traffic; on a sunny day it gleamed like a piece of jewelry.

Qwilleran parked his handsome bike in Polly's office, and Dundee, who had never seen a bicycle in his young life, gave the wheels the sniff test.

Qwilleran said, "He's telling me I need air in the rear tire."

"Have a chair," Polly said. "You'll need to be sitting down to read this." She handed him a business envelope with typed address. With a newsman's lack of personal reaction, he read the letter through—then read it again.

Dear Polly,

It was a privilege and pleasure to meet you Saturday night. I wish we lived in the same town. You would be my role model. Sorry I didn't meet Brutus and Catta.

Here is a snapshot of Jerome taken when he won first prize in a cat fashion show. He was dressed as Santa Claus. I made his costume: a red coat and red cap with white fur trim and a white fur bib hanging around his neck, supposed to be a beard. It was hilariously funny, and he didn't object. Jerome is always calm, cool, and collected.

And now for the bad news—or good, depending on one's point of view. I've broken up with Harvey. I'm still going to call her Aunt Doris and keep in touch. She's so sweet! To tell the truth, I think she likes me more than she does Harvey!

When we got home, Harvey told me I'd have to get rid of Jerome! He hates cats. I said he'd have to get a steady job and/or go to college. He said he wouldn't have to do either because he'll inherit the Ledfield millions or billions.

Well! I took off Aunt Doris's ring and told him I was going to return it to her.

Harvey is sexy and all that, and he has that gorgeous head of hair—but we're all wrong for each other. What do you think, Polly? I don't have anyone to discuss it with, and my family in Indiana wouldn't understand.

> With best wishes,
> Clarissa

"Well . . . What do you think?" Polly asked. "Are you surprised?"

"I'll tell you what I think!" he said. "If my girl-friend dressed up her cat like Santa Claus—with a white fur bib—I'd consider it grounds for murder! . . . No! In any marriage there are periodic disagreements, but to start a lifelong union with a built-in disagreement like theirs would be insanity. She's an ailurophile; he's an ailurophobe. Koko knew it or he wouldn't have gone airborne! I tried to pass it off as a catly game, but Koko is no fool. . . . Sorry to be on my soapbox."

Dundee, who had been courting customers on the selling floor, came running to enjoy the fun.

"I hope my lecture didn't go out over the loudspeakers," Qwilleran said. "What I'm trying to say is this: The only thing Harvey and Clarissa have in common is skiing and I say their so-called engagement was all a pose, on Harvey's part—planned to mislead Doris and Nathan and sew up the inheritance. . . . No matter, the plot backfired. Harvey will have to try again another year." And then he asked casually, "What's on the program at the Bird Club tonight—besides chicken potpie for dinner? I wonder how many pies you can get out of a single chicken?"

"Oh, Qwill!" she remonstrated.

"Do you mind looking after my bike while I go downstairs to see if they have anything new in the old-book department?"

The Edd Smith Place on the lower level had the usual browsers and, as usual, Lisa Compton at the cash register.

"Qwill, I was just thinking about you! We received several boxes of books from Trawnto Beach, including a book I read when I was twelve. I laughed so hard, I rolled on the floor, and my mother thought I was having convulsions. Have you ever read *Three Men in a Boat* by a British humorist published in 1889?"

"No," he said, "and frankly I've never rolled on the floor with laughter."

"You can read it aloud to the cats," Lisa said. "It's a small book, the kind Koko likes to push off the shelf—if you're telling the truth. Lyle and I have never had a cat that pushed books off the shelf, and he says it's a heinous fabrication on your part."

"He's never had a Siamese, that's his problem. . . . I'll take the book. How much? Do I get my money back if I don't roll on the floor?"

. . .

En route to the newspaper office Qwilleran and the British Silverlight received friendly toots from motorists and cheers from admiring pedestrians. One old gentleman shouted in a cracked voice: "Heigh-ho, Silver!"

In front of the Sprenkle Building, a tall stately woman of advanced age stood on the curb and waved. Qwilleran braked his bike abruptly in front of her and said, "Sorry, madam, you'll have to hail a taxi. My license doesn't permit me to transport passengers."

"Qwill, you rascal!" she cried. "You say the most outrageous things with a straight face!"

She was Maggie Sprenkle, one of the town's most active octogenarians, noted for her volunteer work in animal rescue. After her husband's death, she sold their Purple Point property and moved into the Sprenkle Building downtown in order to be closer to her volunteer activities. The ground floor was occupied by insurance and real estate firms; the upper two floors had been transformed into a Victorian palace.

Maggie asked, "Could you come upstairs for a cup of tea? I have something to discuss with you."

"After I've filed my copy at the paper."

"Come around in the rear," she said. "There's room in the back hall to park your bicycle."

In half an hour he returned and rang the bell; a buzzer admitted him and the Silverlight, and he rode to the second floor in a small elevator—all this in a hundred-year-old building with a Victorian palace upstairs. There were crystal chandeliers, plush carpet, patterned with roses, and red walls hung with large paintings in gilt frames.

When she offered him a "nice cup of tea," he said gently, "Somehow, Maggie, a nice cup of tea seems out of sync with a bicycle ride, even on a British one."

She agreed, and served Squunk water with cranberry juice.

Before sitting down at the carved marble-top table, he paid his respects to the five "ladies" from the animal shelter, who sat in five windows overlooking Main Street traffic. They had names like Florence Nightingale, Sarah Bernhardt, Louisa May Alcott, and so forth.

"How's everything at the animal shelter?" he asked.

"Thanks to the K Fund, we've doubled our capacity and hired a second rescue officer. Now, if only we could educate people not to abandon unwanted pets without food, water, or protection from wild animals! A pregnant cat or dog is driven into the country and dropped by the roadside. It breaks my heart! At the shelter, cages are being cleaned and animals bathed by wealthy women volunteers who could be playing afternoon bridge or flying to Chicago for a day's shopping. . . . You know all this, Qwill. You've written columns on it. And you quoted a philosopher: *'It is better to light one small candle than to curse the darkness.'* We try to place as many orphaned animals as we can. That's what I wanted to discuss with you: During the summer, while a lot of out-of-staters are here for reunions, why not have a series of animal auctions?"

Qwilleran gulped. He had been warned. They were going to ask him to be auctioneer! "Sounds like a good idea! I'm sure you could get Foxy Fred to handle it gratis. He would be very good at kidding the audience and pitting bidder against bidder. An out-of-town audience would eat it up!"

"You're very right, Qwill! We've asked him and he's going to do it. And here's what the volunteers suggested. Instead of putting anonymous animals on the block, give them all famous names—like my ladies!"

"Excellent idea!" he said. "Is there anything I can do to help?"

"As a matter of fact . . . yes!" Maggie said. "Could you make up a list of names that are well known? We'd start with kitties."

"With pleasure! They'd be names from literature and legend—no contemporary figures. Politicians or movie stars or others in the news would turn it into a joke. The names can still have a light connotation: Peter Pan, Cholly Knickerbocker, Rosie O'Grady, Goody Two-Shoes. That would be perfect for a female with two white paws."

"Oh, I'm so excited, Qwill! How soon can you give us a list? We have some sharp-witted volunteers who will love fitting the names to the right kitties."

"In fact, Maggie, I'll pay a visit to the shelter. Colors and marking might suggest 'Cinderella' for all white; 'Bonnie Lassie' for an orange marmalade mix; 'Tom Sawyer' for a male with jaunty markings on the head. . . . Enough of this! I could stay here all day! . . . Just let me ask you one question: Do you know the Ledfields?"

He was prompted solely by a free-ranging curiosity that was part of his profession. Maggie's response was more than he anticipated.

"Why, yes! Nathan and Doris were our neighbors in Purple Point! Jeremy and I dined with them often. Nathan is a wonderful man—played the violin. Doris accompanied him on the piano. She's a sweet, retiring person—sad, because she's childless, and the Ledfields have always felt strongly about continuing the bloodline. They have only a nephew in California."

"He visited here last weekend, Maggie, to make sketches of my barn for an architectural project. He's entering college in the fall."

"Really? That will please his aunt and uncle. I believe his name is Harvey. He was here last winter.

Harvey's parents were killed in a car crash on the freeway."

Maggie's cagily secretive expression caused Qwilleran to remark, "A terrible tragedy!"

"Not exactly," she said. "I shouldn't be telling you this, but everyone knows that Nathan's brother was the black sheep of the family—a burden and an embarrassment. When they died, that left Harvey the only heir to the Ledfield fortune, so Nathan sent him a pair of plane tickets, and he visited here with a friend, a personable young man. Nathan found the friend an interesting conversationalist but he was disappointed in Harvey. All the young man could talk about was a glamorous ski lodge in the mountains, which he wanted his uncle to back."

"Any luck?" Qwilleran asked.

"You jest!" Maggie replied. "Nathan considered it a frivolity, and the two youths didn't stay long. Nathan would prefer to put his heir through college."

"Did you meet Harvey? No? It's just as well, Maggie. He's a cat hater. . . . And now I must tear myself away from your fascinating company."

Maggie said, "You're so kind and understanding, Qwill! And always so concerned about people. . . . Don't forget the list of cat names."

On the way out he noticed a small framed photo on a bookshelf. Two couples in a rose garden.

"The handsome one is my Jeremy," Maggie said. "Doris and I are sitting on a bench that Jeremy copied from the one in Monet's *A Garden at Giverny*. My husband did beautiful things with wood. The framed calligraphy is Jeremy's work, too—a quotation from the *Desiderata*: 'With all its sham, drudgery, and broken dreams,/it is still a beautiful world. Be cheerful. Strive to be happy.' "

Maggie added, "Jeremy was unable to walk; he was thrown from a horse when he was a young man. . . . Do you have a copy of the *Desiderata*, Qwill? I have one on my wall, and it's the first thing I see every morning. I have a copy for you, if you have a good place to post it."

He promised to thumbtack it on the bulletin board in his writing studio.

With another look at the photograph in the rose garden, Qwilleran came to several conclusions: Jeremy was indeed handsome and grew beautiful roses. . . . Maggie looked then, as she does now, very much in charge. . . . Nathan was not tall but broad-shouldered, serious—a picture of the concert violinist and keeper of the family dignity. . . . Doris was small and frail and devoted to her husband; she looked at him instead of at the photographer.

Later in the evening, he wrote in his journal:

Friday—Polly and I are making two lists for Maggie: one for males, one for females. I refuse to call them little boys and little girls.

The names, we decided, should be important, well known, strong-sounding, even when reduced to a nickname for everyday use. Volunteers will have to match them up with forty little balls of fur, so we supplied more than enough.

Examples: Rudyard Kipling, Conan Doyle, Lewis and Clark (for twins), Michelangelo, Henry Longfellow, Winslow Homer, Bustopher Jones.

And then: Betsy Ross, Jane Austen, Lorna Doone, Agatha Christie, Cleopatra.

One question: Suppose a sweet little Cinderella grows up to have a personality like Attila the Hun? Does the purchaser get a refund?

EIGHT

It was the second Tuesday in June, and Qwilleran was polishing his second "*Late Great*" for the the "Qwill Pen" when the phone rang.

When Qwilleran answered, he had to chuckle; only his old friend Arch Riker could say "good morning" and make it sound like an accusation.

The editor in chief barked, "Who's Clarissa Moore?"

Assuming a grouchy humor to match, Qwilleran snapped, "Who's calling? And why do you ask?"

"She sent us a job application from California! Gave you as a reference."

"Oh! Her! Yes, I seem to remember, Arch." He was playing a role to the hilt. "She and a friend were visiting the Ledfields in Purple Point. I suppose you know who the Ledfields are?"

"Everyone knows who the Ledfields are! How did you yet involved?"

"Someone suggested I take the young couple to dinner, since she was headed for a career in journalism. She is young—bright, personable. That's all I know." He refrained from mentioning Jerome, the Santa Claus costume, the broken engagement—if it was even a fact.

"She sent tear sheets of her newswriting and feature stories. Pretty good stuff. She's from Indiana, so she'd fit in here."

"Do you have an opening, Arch?"

"That's just it! Jill Handley's taking a year's maternity leave. . . . Is your copy in for today?"

Arch slammed the receiver without waiting for an answer.

Qwilleran had to smile. Everyone in the city room liked Arch and his Grumpy Boss act. He ran a good paper and had a heart of gold. As his wife said, "Arch doesn't want anyone to know how happy he is!"

🐾 Qwilleran finished his profile of Agatha Burns, a teacher who lived to the century mark. He quoted three generations of students:

"I don't know how she did it, but she really made me want to learn."

"Can you imagine? She even made me enjoy Latin."

"When the state Board of Education took Latin off the curriculum, some of us kids staged a protest march. It didn't do any good. After that she taught English and made us get excited about subjects and predicates, and things like gerunds! I haven't thought about a gerund in twenty years."

"My mom went to school in Milwaukee and remembers hating *Silas Marner* and *The Scarlet Letter* . . . but Miss Agatha somehow tricked us into enjoying all those old chestnuts. . . . What was her secret? There must be a secret!"

(Later, when Lisa Compton read the profile, she

said, "I know her secret. She knew how to put herself in the students' shoes; she thought from their viewpoint. Not easy to do!")

After filing his copy at the *Something*, Qwilleran happened upon Gil MacMurchie at the bank. The one was curious about the next parade, and the other was eager to talk about it. They borrowed one of the small conference rooms.

"How's it going?" Qwilleran asked, referring to the Fourth of July parade honoring *Pickax Now*.

"Let me tell you! We had a setback, but not for long. You see, our slogan was '*Everything's Coming Up Roses.*' We were gonna order tons of roses from Down Below, throw them from the floats, drop them from the helicopter! Then somebody reminded us that roses have thorns, and if an eyeball got pricked, the city could get sued."

"They had a point," Qwilleran said.

"So, back to the drawing board. This time we decided on '*Everything's Coming Up Peonies!*' We have peonies in every backyard. The Peony Club has a couple of hundred members! And it won't cost a cent!"

"Smart thinking, Gil! Is there anything I can do?"

"Well, yes. Would the 'Qwill Pen' care to write about the history of peonies? They go back to ancient times and used to have magical powers. There are books in the library, and you could interview the officers of the Peony Club."

(Qwilleran, who was not even sure what a peony looked like, was about to become an authority on yet another subject.) He asked, "Do you know anything about the mansions of Purple Point, Gil?"

"I ought to! Three generations of my family spent their lives crawling between floors of those old hulks. In the nineteenth century, they didn't have bathrooms—only water closets, in spite of all their magnificence."

"Is that so?" Qwilleran mused, remembering that King George III died in his water closet.

Gil went on. "Now all the bedrooms have private baths with walk-in showers and gold faucets! It kept our family busy for three generations. We're not complaining!"

"Do you know the Ledfields' place, Gil?"

"Sure! The Old Manse! They had six bedrooms made into six suites, and the master suite was like a small mansion-within-a-mansion, complete with grand piano. Nice people. They always paid their bills on time . . . and sent their plumber something at Christmas."

That night, Qwilleran and Polly dined at Tipsy's Tavern, a log-built roadhouse north of town, noted for wonderful chicken dinners and memorable brunches. (The owner had his own poultry farm, viewable from the side windows.) The tavern was named after the cat of the original owner. A portrait of Tipsy hung in the main dining room. The staff were all lively women of sixty or more who called Qwilleran "Sonny." He and Polly went there often.

Tonight they were seated in a quiet alcove for two, overlooking the poultry yards.

Polly said, "Last night Arch had a dinner meeting somewhere, and Mildred and I had a nice supper at their place, chattering like magpies all the time. Then we had tea and cookies on the deck, and it was so peaceful and pleasant, we didn't say a word. Then suddenly Mildred said something I didn't understand."

"Can you tell me what it was?" he asked. "Or is it a female secret?"

The words were, as Polly recalled them, "The time of many murders is after midnight."

Polly explained that there are times when one is alone and contented—or with friends who are quiet and happy, and no one is talking—then suddenly you want to say something but have nothing to say.

She paused to await Qwilleran's reaction.

"Hmmm," he murmured thoughtfully—a reaction well known to his friends.

"Mildred said it was a practice sentence when she was learning to type in high school, and it drifts back into her head when it's completely empty."

"I can understand," he said. "I have a Dickens quotation that serves the same purpose."

It was from *A Tale of Two Cities*: "It is a far, far better thing that I do, than I have ever done."

Then Polly confessed hers. "Nothing will come

of nothing." She had inherited it from her father, who was a Shakespeare scholar. Qwilleran knew the play: *King Lear*. How could he forget?

At that moment one of the grandmotherly waitresses bustled into the room. "Do you kiddies want dessert?"

The house specialty was bread pudding with a sauce made with maple syrup from their own trees.

On the way home Polly said, "Everyone's talking about your 'Late Great' column on Agatha Burns."

"I had a warm letter from her niece, who lives in Ittibittiwassee Estates. She sent me one of Agatha's books. It came by motorcycle messenger. He also almost fell off his bike when he saw Koko hopping around in the kitchen window. The famous Koko! He could hardly wait to tell his wife that he had seen Cool Koko in person."

"What was the book?" she asked.

"Hawthorne's *Mosses from an Old Manse*."

"How appropriate! The Ledfields call their place the Old Manse!"

"When I put the book on the coffee table, Koko

immediately sat on it. I told him he had good taste in literature, and he blinked his eyes."

The next afternoon, as Qwilleran was reading Nathaniel Hawthorne to two unsuspecting Siamese, he had a phone call from Thornton Haggis at the art center.

"Got a couple of minutes? I've got some interesting news."

"I've just made some fresh coffee, Thorn. Why don't you trot up here."

The visitor admired the cats, praised the coffee, had some good words to say about Hawthorne.

"Well, don't keep me in suspense," Qwilleran said.

"Do you know the Kennebeck Knitter?"

"She's doing a sweater for me."

"Do you know about her predictions?"

Qwilleran said, "Don't tell me the next parade is going to be rained out! Gil MacMurchie will have a stroke."

"Worse than that! Her predictions have always

been about natural disasters. Before the last parade, she foresaw man-made crimes for the first time and she still sees it. Shooting and poisoning! She's not talkin' about BB guns and tainted potato salad, but real crime! Man-made, not weather-made!"

"Hmmm," Qwilleran mused. What could he say?

Thorn said, "Well, they're doing a new show at the gallery. They need me to climb the ladder. Thanks for the coffee."

NINE

While Qwilleran waited for a calamity to prove his theory, that everything was going too well for *Pickax Now* (he was right, of course, but proof would come later), Clarissa arrived, as reported in his private journal.

Tuesday—Clarissa has arrived.

No fuss, no muss. She's a real newswoman—independent; knows her way around; no need for welcoming assistance. Her curls and dimples are misleading.

———————————

So we learn that she and Jerome and luggage arrived by plane, then drove an airport rental car to the Winston Park apartments, where she had reserved a unit by phone. Her first consideration was to stock up on cat food and litter for Jerome's commode, which apparently came with them from California, although *how* is not quite clear.

Although not due to report until next week, she went to the paper and introduced herself, shaking hands, lining up a desk in the feature department and even accepting an assignment for Monday morning. I'd say she's off to a good start. Joe Bunker just called to say he's giving a pizza party for our blond bombshell on Sunday night.

Qwilleran was not surprised to receive a phone call from Wetherby. "She's here! She's here!"

He replied with sly punctilio. "To whom are you referring?"

"You know who I mean! And I'm giving a pizza party for her Sunday night. Could you pick her up? She has an apartment at Winston Park."

"Am I invited to the party, or am I employed to do chauffeur service?"

"You're not only invited, you donkey, but I expect you to contribute to the entertainment. How about reciting some of your cat limericks?"

"If you'll play '*Kitten on the Keys*' without exceeding the speed limit."

Following this good-old-boy repartee, Qwilleran phoned Clarissa to make arrangements. "I hope you like pizza," he said.

"Doesn't everyone? What time?"

"Six-thirty. Come as you are."

"Will you come in for a minute to say hello to Jerome? He's dying to meet you."

"Sure . . . but tell him not to dress up. His old blue fur will do."

Qwilleran had other things on his mind besides Wetherby's pizza party. He had two columns to write for the "Qwill Pen" . . . perform another Sunday matinee of *The Big Burning* (three down and only ten to go) . . . make an appearance at a family reunion . . . and keep his own family well fed and happy. If the Siamese felt neglected, they had succinct ways of expressing their displeasure.

So he cubed some meat loaf from Robin O'Dell Catering and arranged it attractively on two plates. While they dined, he entertained them with an impromptu parody of Gelett Burgess's wacky verse:

> *I've never seen a purple cat.*
> *I never hope to see one.*
> *But you can bet your breakfast that*
> *I'd rather see than be one.*

His listeners regarded him in perplexity, as if questioning his sanity. Their catly psyche was not being pricked.

Of the seven family reunions scheduled for Pickax, Qwilleran chose the Ogilvie-Fugtree gathering. He had known Mitch Ogilvie ever since the young bachelor had been manager of a rural museum in North Middle Hummock; Qwilleran had met Kristi Fugtree when the K Fund helped her register her ancestral home as an historic place.

Now they were married and starting a family. She was a goat farmer; Mitch had learned how to make goat cheese. They lived in the house that Kristi's great-grandfather, Captain Fugtree, built when he returned from the wars: a tall brick mansion in the Victorian style—with a tower. According to legend, a "maiden in distress" once flung herself from the tower "on a dark and stormy night."

When Qwilleran drove to the reunion on Saturday afternoon, he could hear sounds of revelry in the quiet countryside long before he came upon the scene.

His first impression upon arrival was one of color, quite unlike the somber aspect of the farm in previous years, when Kristi's entire herd of goats had been tragically wiped out.

Now the grass seemed greener, the old brick redder, and the colorful attire of folks on holiday resembled a garden in motion.

Dozens of celebrators were laughing, jabbering, running around, playing games, guzzling soft drinks.

Men were pitching horseshoes, young people were playing badminton. Their elders huddled in lawn chairs, and his tape recorder picked up chatter like this:

"He's had several promotions, so they're doing all right financially."

"Do you like the color Helen dyed her hair?"

"I didn't see you at Gail's wedding; it was lovely!"

"Isn't that radio rather loud?"

"I never thought Kristi would have children, but the twins are adorable!"

"Max and Theo arrived together. Does that mean they're not feuding?"

"Uncle Morry bought their plane tickets."

"That dear man! So much money and he can't enjoy it."

"He won't be with us much longer."

"Why is Morry so good to those boys? They have no ambition."

"Morry says the rest of us have everything we want."

"Have you seen the Wilsons' new house? It's very modern!"

"Their son went to college on a basketball scholarship."

"Laura's talking about a divorce. Too bad."

"How do you feel about goats? Kristi's mad about them."

"She says goat's milk is good for the digestion."

"I should try it. Isn't that radio awfully loud?"

Qwilleran asked Kristi how they handled overnight accommodations. She said, "The kids like the tents in the backyard, and the older folks sleep in the rooms upstairs. We've an elevator now. Others shack up with Ogilvie families around the county."

"Who has traveled the farthest?"

"A Fugtree family from Texas."

"Do you make an effort to entertain them?"

"As you probably know, Mitch is a good story-teller, and I introduce everyone to the goats, who are really sweet and sociable. Also, Mitch explains cheese making.

"And then, you've probably noticed the games at the picnic tables: cards, Parcheesi, checkers, jig-saw puzzles—"

"Does everyone get along?"

"The kids have a few squabbles, but Mitch is great at handling them. He's also organized a committee to figure out how the Ogilvies and the Fugtrees can leave the town of Pickax some useful memento of their visit here."

"Any ideas yet?"

"Not so far."

Qwilleran circulated. Many out-of-towners knew who he was and wanted to be photographed with him. It was the moustache they loved.

He enjoyed talking to two young women, sisters, who played mandolin and flute. Then there were two young men, cousins, who asked him about rabbit hunting in Moose County. And Kristi said the caterer would make hasenpfeffer if they brought back any rabbits.

When the hunters left for the woods, Qwilleran left to go home and feed the cats. As he told Polly later, "I didn't want to be there when two grinning hunters returned, clutching rabbits by the ears."

On the way home, Qwilleran stopped at the bookstore. He and Polly had decided to forgo their Saturday night dinner date and musicale—this, in anticipation of a busy weekend.

He said, "Joe has asked me to pick up Clarissa for his party, but Judd Amhurst will take her home. So you and I can finish the evening with a little Mozart and Berlioz at your place."

She agreed. "What did you think of the Ogilvie-Fugtree reunion?"

"Not bad. I can make it sound better than it was."

Polly said, "I'm excited about tomorrow afternoon; I've seen the Big Burning show a total of four times over the years, but I always weep when you talk about the father who tried to save his two small children."

Qwilleran admitted that he choked up himself, no matter how many times he had read that passage.

In the script the radio announcer said, "And then there was a father who tried to save his two small children, but he couldn't because his right arm was burned off. Burned off! He had to choose between them!"

There were a few minutes of silence, and then Polly said, "Don't forget the Heirloom Auction next Saturday. Have you thought of anything you can donate?"

"Only the twistle-twig rocker, but I donated it

to a charity auction once before and had to buy it back because Koko went on a hunger strike. The myth is that anyone sitting in it will think great thoughts."

"Where do you keep it?" Polly asked. "I haven't seen it for years!"

"Well, the barn interior looks best with no-nonsense contemporary. I keep the twistle-twig in the cats' apartment. Yum Yum gives it a wide berth, but Koko likes the bowl-shaped seat. Well, see you tomorrow after the show."

As Qwilleran drove back to the barn, it occurred to him that the twistle-twig rocker might account for Koko's remarkable psychic ability. Qwilleran had always attributed the cat's foresight to his sixty whiskers—sixty instead of the standard forty-eight; but perhaps that crafty little animal had also been sitting in the bowl-shaped seat of the twistle-twig and thinking extraordinary thoughts.

The "Smart Koko" was dancing in the kitchen window when Qwilleran drove into the barnyard; it meant there was a message on the answering machine.

A man's voice said, "Qwill! Don't run anything

in the paper about the reunion! We have some bad trouble here! This is Mitch."

Unable to believe his ears, Qwilleran listened to the message a second time. At the same moment Koko, who was right at his elbow, stretched his neck and uttered a howl that would chill the blood.

It started in his lower depths and ended in an unearthly shriek! It was not the first time Qwilleran had heard Koko's death howl, and he knew what it meant. Wrongful death . . . someone . . . somewhere.

Linking Mitch's cryptic message and Koko's doleful one, Qwilleran refrained from phoning the farmhouse for more particulars; he could imagine the frenzy that had replaced the happy scene.

Instead, he took a shortcut; he phoned the newspaper.

TEN

🐾 The newspaper published no edition over the weekend, but a deskman was always on duty in the city room, answering the phone and listening to the squawking of the police-band radio.

Qwilleran recognized the voice that came on the wire. "Is this Barry? Qwill here. Any trouble reported in the North Middle Hummocks? I just received a queer tip."

"Yeah, the sheriff and his dog are searching for a missing person. Rabbit hunter. Probably some guy at a family reunion got lost in the woods."

"Or got shot by another rabbit hunter," Qwilleran said, thinking of Koko's anguished howl.

"Ain't it the truth, Qwill! Out where we live, there are so many rifle shots in the woods, come weekend, that it sounds like the Fourth of July. How they can avoid shooting each other is a mystery. . . . Hold it! . . ."

Qwilleran waited. But both he and Koko had the answers.

The cynical deskman came back on the line.

"What'd I tell ya? Another rabbit hunter bit the dust. Only ten thousand left. Gotta hang up."

Qwilleran preferred not to picture the scene at the goat farm, and he regretted that his friends would be deprived of good news coverage. As for himself, his time and recording tape would not be wasted. He could write an anonymous description of an ideal family reunion, where all the adults are happy and all the children are well behaved and all the conversation is upbeat and all the food is delicious.

On the other hand, he could cut his losses and scrap his notes. He and Polly discussed it on the phone that night. She had worked at the bookstore so that her assistant could entertain visiting relatives. She needed to rest up before a busy Sunday: church, then lunch with the Rikers, after which they would go to the Big Burning show downtown, and then there would be Wetherby's supper party.

Clarissa had dropped into the bookstore and was thrilled with her new job and looking forward to the pizza party but was worried about the health of Aunt Doris and Uncle Nathan. Clarissa wanted to return the valuable ring and explain the breakup with Harvey, but she could talk only with a housekeeper.

Qwilleran listened to it all with appropriate reactions but contributed no newsbites of his own. He merely said he would like to go into a trance on Sunday before switching identities with an imaginary nineteenth-century newscaster. He said he would see Polly at Joe's party.

"*À bientôt*," she said.

"*À bientôt*."

🐾 Once more Qwilleran played to a full house on Sunday afternoon. The audience reaction was always the same:

A woman sobbed audibly as she listened to accounts of family tragedies and remembered the stories told in her own family.

A man blew his nose loudly over the plight of the father trying to save his two children.

There was heavy silence as the audience pictured hundreds of victims taking refuge in the new brick courthouse, the same building where one now went to pay property taxes or apply for a marriage license.

"Devastating" . . . "unbelievable" . . . "heartbreaking" were the words Qwilleran heard when he appeared in the lobby after the show.

He was glad to return to the barn and spend a quiet hour or two with the Siamese before leaving for Winston Park to pick up Clarissa.

When he arrived at her apartment, she was in a festive mood, but a cat of imposing size was sitting calmly in the center of the middle seat cushion of the sofa.

"Hail to thee, Sir Jerome!" Qwilleran said with a grand gesture.

The cat observed him with large golden eyes and without a flicker of a whisker.

To Clarissa, Qwilleran said, "Magnificent creature! What language does he speak?" He was accustomed to the Siamese with their voluble responses and expressive gestures.

"He's awed by your moustache."

She explained, "I don't know why he always sits in the exact middle of a chair or cushion or rug—or anything."

"He's a Centrist," Qwilleran said with authority. "Many cats are Centrists. If they were humans, they'd be halfway between Republicans and Democrats."

Before they left Qwilleran complimented Jerome on his blue coat (which he still considered gray)... and slyly complimented Clarissa on her *gray* pantsuit (which was obviously blue).

Qwilleran noted that his passenger was carrying a large satchel-type handbag, reminding him of Thelma Thackery. Was this California style? He avoided dropping the usual masculine quips. (Bring your own dinner? Planning to stay overnight?) Later he would learn what it contained.

En route to the party he told her what new faces she would meet: Connie Constable was a vet at the pet hospital, especially good with cats . . . and Judd Amhurst was a retired engineer and now manager of special events at the bookstore.

Then he remarked, "I hear you have settled in at the paper."

"Yes, and everyone is so friendly! Roger MacGillivray introduced me around. . . . Is he married?"

"Not only married but father of three, whom he's helping to homeschool. You've met John Bushland—prizewinning photographer. Likes to be called Bushy. He and Roger and I were once marooned on a deserted island in a horrendous storm. The three of us are bonded for life."

During cocktails and while waiting for the pizza delivery, Wetherby outdid himself at the piano, playing Chopin's "*Minute Waltz*." Then Qwilleran was induced to compose an impromptu limerick about Jerome:

An out-of-town cat named Jerome
Says, "I never wanted to roam.
There's not enough sun
And the mice are no fun.
Show me the way to go home."

Then Judd asked Qwilleran if he could write limericks about dogs.

"I just happen to have one with me." He drew an index card from his pocket, having expected Judd to bring up the subject sooner or later. The card read:

There once was a hound with an itch
Who didn't know which end was which.
But he was no fool;
He went off to school,
And learned: Every dog has his niche.

Eventually the subject of the Heirloom Auction took the spotlight. Everyone agreed it was for a good cause and wanted to participate.

"Clever kids, those students of Burgess's," said

Wetherby. "They get you coming or going—or both. I donate my grandpappy's moustache cup—then go to the auction and bid on some other grandpappy's shaving mug."

Polly said, "I'm not in the market for any more *objects* but I'm donating a lot of my in-laws' collection."

Clarissa said she would attend for the thrill of bidding on something. "The only item I have to donate is nothing that anyone could possibly want. I hang onto it only because my grandmother acquired it when she was young."

"What is it?" everyone asked at once.

"I've brought it to show you. Tell me what you think."

There was silence as she reached for her large handbag and withdrew a roll of something like a diploma. Tied with ribbon, it was about three inches in diameter and a foot long. When unrolled, it proved to be a three-foot advertisement for a breakfast cereal.

Sheepishly she said, "A poster from a Detroit trolley car." She waited, and when there was no comment, said, "It's really sort of pretty and in good condition. It's been rolled up for sixty years. When my grandmother was young, she used to ride to work on the trolley car, which was so crowded that passengers had to stand in the aisles and hang onto leather straps, and stare at the ads that filled the space above the windows. . . . I don't know how Grandma happened to acquire this one. I suppose it was a souvenir of many hours of straphanging."

Qwilleran said, "You should donate it, Clarissa, and Joe and I will bid against each other for it—have a little fun. I'll bid the highest and take it home to hang in the cats' apartment. It'll go with their twistle-twig rocker."

Wetherby said, "The poster would make a better presentation if framed. I know a guy in Horseradish who'll frame it for nothing—just to go along with a gag!"

The others were laughing and cheering them on and Judd said he'd make a few bids for it himself. "Is this what they call shill bidding? Is it ethical?"

"In this case, it's just a stunt," Qwilleran said, "and the proceeds go to a good cause. We'll get Foxy Fred to make it the first item on the block. It'll wake up the audience. Get them in the spirit of the occasion. . . . The trick will be, Joe, to decide how high to go. To make it a sensation, it should be an outrageous figure, which the K Fund will cover, of course."

During the evening there was plenty of conversation about cats. Jet Stream swaggered among the guests and accepted compliments and crumbs of cheese. Clarissa showed her snapshot of Jerome, the only British Shorthair in the county, she thought. Dr. Connie, newly divorced, had acquired a marmalade, related to Dundee, the bibliocat at the bookstore.

Polly said that Brutus and Catta had made friends with a wild rabbit, who came out of the woods daily to commune with them through the window wall.

Qwilleran told them that Koko and Yum Yum were studying crows aiming for a degree in corvidology. He refrained from reporting Koko's death howl in the case of the missing rabbit hunter.

Before the evening was over, Wetherby played Mendelssohn's *Presto Agitato*, which required incredible nimbleness of fingering. Judd, the engineer, insisted that the music required a pianist to play a thousand notes a minute. Clarissa, the journalist, checked to see if Wetherby had six fingers on each hand.

Polly said, "Joe, why aren't you on the concert stage?"

"I'm not good enough," he said. "And I believe if you can't be good, be fast."

The party broke up early. Before leaving with Judd, Clarissa whispered to Qwilleran that she wanted to talk with him about the Ledfields. "Anytime!" he said. Wetherby took her streetcar poster and promised to have it framed overnight.

🐾 Back at the barn, Qwilleran phoned the police chief at home. "Andy, are you interested in talking about rabbit hunters over a thimbleful of Scotch?"

"I'll talk about anything over a wee dram!"

Andrew Brodie lived in the neighborhood and drove into the barnyard within minutes. The Siamese rushed to the kitchen window, either recognizing the sound of the chief's motor or reading Qwilleran's mind. They knew the burly Scotsman with the loud voice. Over the years he had progressed from suspicious stranger to admiring friend, calling them "that smart Koko" and "my little sweetheart." Yum Yum was not only allowed to untie his shoelaces but was expected to do so.

Brodie made himself at home, sitting at the snack bar, pouring a large "thimbleful" of Scotch and cutting a slice of cheese.

He said, "M' wife and some ladies from the church saw your show this afternoon. She said they all had a good cry. It's not the first time they've seen it. How does it feel to give it in the opera house?"

"Better than church basements, school gyms, and county parks."

Brodie commented on the tastiness of the cheese, a Manchego from Spain. He said he'd never heard of it but it was good!

Finally Qwilleran said, "I hear there was a disturbance in North Middle Hummock yesterday."

"What do you know about it?"

"I was there to cover the Ogilvie-Fugtree family reunion, but by the time I got home, there was a message on my phone, canceling the story. I phoned the paper and learned someone from the party had been killed while hunting rabbits."

The chief took a swig of his drink before saying, "Off the record, it looks like homicide. A member of the party was arrested on suspicions. That's all I'm tellin'."

Qwilleran said, "That smart Koko, who's gobbling crumbs of cheese that you 'accidentally' drop, probably knows more than the sheriff does." He referred to the cat's death howl at five-fifteen, the day the hunter was reported missing.

"What else does that smart cat know?"

"That's all I'm tellin', Andy."

ELEVEN

On Monday morning, while feeding the cats, Qwilleran received a phone call from Mitch Ogilvie. "Qwill, I owe you an apology!"

"About what?"

"You wasted a whole afternoon of your valuable time."

"My time is never wasted, Mitch. Everything is fodder for the 'Qwill Pen' or even for a future novel! Who knows? However, I'm curious to know what actually happened Saturday afternoon."

Mitch said, "I'm going to town for supplies. Could you meet me somewhere?"

"How about coming to the barn? You know where it is."

In half an hour the goat farmer's van pulled into the barnyard, and Qwilleran went out to welcome his longtime friend.

Mitch handed him a foil-wrapped package. "Some goat cheese. They say it's good for allergies and digestion."

Indoors, coffee was served in the living area, where two sumptuously cushioned sofas right-angled around a large square coffee table, facing the fireplace cube.

"I don't mind telling you," Mitch said, "it's good to get away from the celebrating crowd—or what's left of it. A lot of them went home early because of the . . . incident. Did you meet the two young fellows who went rabbit hunting, Qwill? I still can't believe what happened."

"Who were the two rabbit hunters? Where were they from?"

"Well, it's quite a story. They're cousins, Max and Theo. Both living in Texas. They have a rich uncle, who has named them his sole heirs because other branches of the family have all the money they need."

"Did the rich uncle come to the reunion?"

"No. Uncle Morry is an invalid and never travels. . . . Now Theo is dead, and Max is suspected. The police say it was homicide—not an accident— and they must have reasons."

Qwilleran asked, "Were they both good hunters?"

"Well, I don't know. It was Max's idea, and Theo seemed to go along."

"How much do you know for a fact?"

"Well, Max says they decided to split up in the woods, one on each side of the creek. They invented a code for keeping in touch. Two whistles meant got-a-rabbit. Three whistles quitting-returning-to-farm. Max never heard any signals from Theo, although he heard a lot of shotgun fire on the other side of the creek."

Qwilleran asked, "Is one side of the creek better hunting than the other?"

"The west bank," Mitch said, "and Max gave that side to Theo, who's a less experienced hunter.

When he came back alone I was ready to lead a search party, but Kristi said Theo might be hurt, and there was no time to waste, so we called the sheriff. After all, it was Saturday, and the locals would be out to bag their Sunday dinner."

Qwilleran asked, "How are the members of the family reacting?"

"They're not talking, but they all have guarded expressions, as if they know something. Kristi says Max and Theo have always been at loggerheads."

"Do you have an opinion, Mitch—off the record?"

"Well, you can't help thinking that the surviving heir will double his inheritance."

At that moment Koko, who had been on the balcony and listening—fell or jumped onto one of the sofa cushions next to the visitor. He landed close enough to make Mitch yelp!

"Bad cat!" Qwilleran scolded, and Koko left the scene in a guilty scramble.

"Sorry!" Qwilleran said. "That's the second time he's done that."

"That's all right," Mitch said. "He just wants to

be included in the conversation. Or it's time for his lunch. . . . I'm leaving, anyway. Errands to do."

"Give Kristi my best wishes. She's looking wonderful, and the twins are a credit to you both."

He walked with his guest to the barnyard and then returned to face an impudent-looking Koko on the bar top with legs splayed, eyes like a pair of daggers, and tail lashing! What was he saying?

In mid-afternoon Qwilleran's reading was interrupted by a phone call from Clarissa: "Qwill, do you have time to see me? I could drive over after work."

"Of course."

"See you at five-thirty."

The car that drove into the barnyard was a green almost-new two-door sedan.

"From Gippel's showroom!" she announced. "Scott Gippel himself waited on me and gave me a fantastic deal when I mentioned the *Something*. I also dropped your name, and that didn't hurt. I hope you don't mind."

"What did you think of Scott Gippel?"

"He's immense! He looks like Henry the Eighth!"

"But he's a good citizen, involved in everything, and always speaks his mind. It's not always printable, but it's honest."

He said, "What would you like to drink? How about a glass of Moose County Madness?"

"What is it?" she asked warily.

"Squunk water with a jigger of cranberry juice and a sprinkle of grated lemon peel."

"Okay. I'm feeling reckless. . . . Where are the cats?"

"In the gazebo. Go out and talk to them, and I'll take the tray out there."

A few moments later, when he arrived with a tray, both cats were on Clarissa's lap.

"They're more gregarious than Jerome," she said.

Qwilleran raised his glass. "Here's to a happy career 400 miles north of everywhere! . . . Now don't keep me in suspense; what was your first assignment?"

"I am thrilled! I'm to research and write a four-part series on the Heirloom Auction!"

"Congratulations! That calls for dinner at the Old Grist Mill."

"I'd love it! Will I be welcome in my work clothes?"

"The press is always welcome, Clarissa—anywhere, at any time. It makes up for being underpaid. I'll go in and phone for a table. You put the cats in that canvas totebag and bring them indoors."

As they drove to the restaurant in his SUV, he said, "Being from Indiana, no doubt you know what a grist mill is."

"A flour mill?" she asked hesitantly.

"Yes—a big stone building with a mill wheel that used to be powered by a rushing stream, long since dried up. Now it's owned by a young woman from Chicago; the interior design is tasteful; the menu is sophisticated; the maître d' is six-feet-eight. His name is Derek Cuttlebrink; he's from the town of Wildcat, and I've known him ever since he was a six-foot-two busboy."

At the restaurant they were greeted by the owner, Liz Hart, who seemed to have a particular fondness for Qwilleran.

He made the introductions, and the two women

immediately warmed up to each other, as he knew they would.

Derek looked approvingly at the dimpled, curly-haired blonde.

"Is he married?" she whispered to Qwilleran after Derek had handed them menus and left the table.

"No," was the answer, "but he and his boss are . . . a *couple* who share a condo in Indian Village."

When drink orders were taken, Clarissa ordered a Moose County Madness, which had to be explained because Qwilleran had coined the name only two hours before.

Then food orders were placed, and Clarissa said she would like something they don't have in California.

With a wink at Qwilleran, the maître d' solemnly rose to his full height and with tongue in cheek recommended Bloody Creek frog legs or Wildcat stew. "They're not on the menu, but they're very good."

Clarissa ordered lamb chops. But Qwilleran called the man's bluff and ordered the frog legs.

"Good choice," Derek said and wrote it on his pad. "How would you like them done?"

Slyly, Qwilleran said, "The same way the chef prepared them the last time, Derek. They were excellent."

But the game was not yet over, and the ball was in Derek's court, Qwilleran mused with satisfaction.

Two minutes later, Derek returned, looking apologetic. "I'm terribly sorry, Mr. Q, but we've just served the last order of frog legs. They're very popular."

Clarissa listened solemnly, then asked, "Why is it called Bloody Creek?"

"No one knows, except that the bridge is the scene of auto accidents, caused by an S-curve in the highway. . . . Now tell me about your first day on the job."

"Well, first I interviewed Burgess Campbell in his home. They're all gingerbread houses on Pleasant Street! I was amazed!"

"It's properly called Carpenter Gothic," he corrected her, "and the street has been featured in national design magazines. The houses were built by an early Campbell, who was a builder of four-masted schooners."

"Everything here is so interesting," she cried.

"Did you meet Burgess's guide dog?"

"Yes, and he's so professional! No sniffing or tail wagging. When I told him he was a *good dog*, he looked as if he was thinking, 'Watch your language, lady.'"

"Burgess—he told me to call him that because there are hundreds of Campbells in the county—gave me a good interview, explaining the why, what, and who of the Heirloom Auction. Then I requested a photographer from the paper and John Bushland met me at the Feed-and-Seed building, where the donated items are being collected. The auction itself will be held in the community hall downtown."

Clarissa was so excited, she was forgetting her lamb chops.

She said, "Each of my four features will have a large photo of some important item in the sale—along with my byline and mug shot, and I'm going to send my whole series to my adviser at school. She'll be impressed. I know it's not the *Los Angeles Times*, but it's a beginning."

During the meal, her gaze wandered as the tall,

lanky black-suited maître d' moved among the tables.

"Isn't Liz Hart rather young to own a restaurant, Qwill?"

He explained. "She was a poor-young-rich-girl in Chicago who escaped a domineering mother, discovered Pickax and Derek, the most popular bachelor in town."

Clarissa said that it sounded like a fairy tale.

"It does, and everyone is waiting for the happy ending."

"Is Cuttlebrink Derek's real name?"

"Absolutely! There's a town called Wildcat that's full of Cuttlebrinks."

"Really? Where did it get its name?"

"Railroad trains go wildcatting through small towns."

"Oh! What does that mean?"

"Going too fast in a controlled-speed zone."

"Oh!"

Her cryptic syllables fascinated him, and he waited for the next question. She was, after all, a journalist.

"Before you forget, Clarissa, what did you want to tell me about the Ledfields?"

"Yes, something strange is happening at the Old Manse. I phoned to make an appointment and return her fabulous ring, but I can't talk to anyone except a secretary, who says they are unwell. When Harvey and I were there, they seemed in good health. Am I getting the runaround? What do you think I should do?"

He was getting twinges of suspicion in his upper lip. Actually, Qwilleran had not been comfortable with the situation for some time—not since Koko had dropped on Harvey's head. It was something the cat had never done before! Then, a second time, he had dropped on the sofa alongside Mitch Ogilvie. Was there a connection?

All of this flashed through Qwilleran's mind in answer to Clarissa's question.

He said, "I can understand your concern, but don't let it interfere with your concentration on your new job. My advice would be to send Doris a handsome get-well card and enclose a note explaining what happened to your 'engagement' and tell her you want to return her ring. Ask how she wants you to go about it. Enclose your phone numbers at home and at the office. Send the card by motorcycle messenger."

When they ordered dessert—cherries jubilee for her, strawberry shortcake for him—Derek flamed the cherries at the table with a flourish that impressed Clarissa.

"He has style," she whispered.

"He's an actor in the theatre club," Qwilleran explained. "He's currently playing the villain in *Billy the Kid*. There are press passes available, if you're interested."

So it went—an evening of excitement for the newcomer. On the way back to the barnyard she was quiet, however, and just before she left in her new little used car she said, "Qwill, I've had a wonderful time, and you've been so kind that I feel guilty. There are things I should explain. It's easier to say in writing, so I left a note for you—on the top of the bar."

Clarissa drove away, and Qwilleran hurried indoors faster than usual. . . . There was no note, but Koko sat on the bar, looking guilty.

It was not until Tuesday morning that Qwilleran

brought the stepladder to the living room and found Clarissa's letter, complete with fang marks, on the top of the fireplace cube.

Dear Qwill,

You and Polly have been so kind and helpful that I owe you an explanation. I was never engaged to Harvey; I was part of his scam to get money from his uncle for a ski lodge. It didn't work, and I should never have taken part in it. But if I hadn't, I wouldn't be here, working for the *Something* and meeting so many wonderful people.

Clarissa

TWELVE

🐾 Another week! Another *"Late Great"* profile for the "Qwill Pen" column. Osmond Hasselrich had been the founder and majordomo of the law firm known as HBB&A. When Qwilleran inherited the Klingenschoen fortune, it was old Mr. Hasselrich who helped him establish the K Fund.

Qwilleran still remembered how the attorney served tea before commencing any business meeting in his mahogany-paneled office. His secretary would bring teapot and cups on a silver tray, and the elderly gentleman insisted on pouring the tea with his trembling hands into his grandmother's Victorian porcelain teacups.

Did anyone know what had happened to those precious teacups that rattled in their saucers when the old man passed them to his clients?

Lisa Compton had done the research on Hasselrich. Qwilleran labored to give balance to the thousand-word profile: Osmond Hasselrich had been a pioneer's son . . . educated by the largesse of grandparents in Philadelphia . . . a struggling young lawyer in the straggling town of Pickax . . . his life included half a century of hard work and genuine concern for his clients . . . eventually he had three partners and a richly paneled office.

A researcher's note said, "Qwill, rumor has it that Fanny Klingenschoen had a torrid romance with Osmond before he went to law school and before she became a belly dancer in Atlantic City, but I don't think you want to mention that.—Lisa."

Qwilleran filed his Tuesday copy by motorcycle messenger, leaving him time for desk chores. Then at two o'clock he walked down the trail to the back road, where there was a rural mailbox and a newspaper sleeve. Clarissa's first feature story would be on page one. How much space would they give her? How big a byline? What position?

He well remembered his first assignment on a Chicago paper. It was buried in a back section; the copy was butchered; his name was misspelled. But that was Chicago, and this was Pickax.

The first of four installments on the Heirloom Auction appeared on the front page above the fold. And the illustration was a large photo of an Abraham Lincoln portrait—in copper—actually a printer's copperplate from which thousands of black-and-white prints had been pulled. There was also a teaser, saying, "Watch for another pedigreed antiquity in tomorrow's *Something*."

Clarissa would be walking on air, and Qwilleran could enjoy her pleasure vicariously.

He was sitting on the porch of the art center and was not surprised when volunteer Thornton Haggis burst out of the building saying, "How long have you been sitting here? We charge for parking!"

"How much do you want for the bench? I'll buy it," Qwilleran retorted.

Thorn sat down alongside him, and Qwilleran said, "Do you remember the young couple visiting me, who bought one of your wood turnings? You entertained them with local history. This is the girl. She's living here now."

The historian looked at the mug shot and remembered them very well. "They are related to the Ledfields."

"And thereby hangs a tale, Thorn. The Ledfields have become quite reclusive, I hear."

"Oh, they never made the big social scene, Qwill. They're one of the last fine-old-families worthy of the name, and I think it weighs heavily on Nathan that the Ledfields are dying out. His brother, who was killed in an accident recently, was a blight on the family name; I don't know about the man's son. Is he the one with all the hair who came down here and bought one of my bowls?"

"He's the one!"

"Wel-l-l!" His inflections expressed plenty.

"Doris Ledfield was on Polly's board of directors at the library for a short time, Thorn, but she resigned."

"Yes, Doris is sweet but shy. She worships the ground Nathan walks on. In fact there is a story that I wouldn't repeat to anyone but you, Qwill. When Doris found out she was barren, she offered Nathan a divorce so he could continue the bloodline elsewhere. It's to his credit that he was appalled at the suggestion. Oh, he's a gentleman! And he lives by a rigorous code of ethics."

"Have you heard him play the violin?"

"He could be on the concert stage, Qwill! . . . Excuse me." Thornton was called indoors to the phone, and Qwilleran walked back up the lane more slowly and thoughtfully than he had walked down.

Around six P.M. Qwilleran phoned Maggie Sprenkle at home, when she would be having a bowl of hot chicken soup and a green leafy salad after a hard day at the animal shelter. Her dining table seated six, and he could imagine her five ladies keeping her company, one on each chair, sitting quietly. In a Victorian palace, even the cats behaved like royalty. They never even spoke until spoken to—and then only with ladylike mews.

When assured that he was not interrupting dinner, Qwilleran asked, "Did you see the spread on the auction in today's paper?"

"I did indeed! Who wrote it? The name is new to me."

"The new feature writer from California, who has just arrived with her cat, a British Shorthair. She'll be assigned to cover the kitty auction, no doubt, and she'll do a good job. Clarissa would feel honored to meet your ladies, having admired them from across the street."

"How did she happen to find Pickax, Qwill?"

"Interesting story! The Ledfields' nephew brought her here as his fiancée, and since he had given her no ring, Doris gave her one of her diamonds. However, Harvey turned out to be a cat hater, and Clarissa dropped him."

"I can well imagine," Maggie said vehemently.

"But she liked it here, and the newspaper was glad to get her. However, a problem has arisen; she'd like to return the ring, and she can't reach

Doris. Only secretaries and housekeepers come to the phone."

Maggie said, "There's one thing about Nathan Ledfield that Jeremy and I had to learn. He's a perfectionist—and very proper. Everything has to be just so! To appear in public with the sniffles and a box of tissues—as I sometimes do—would be unthinkable for Nathan, and Doris has to live by his rules. So . . . when they're suffering from allergies—the polite word for coughs and sneezes—it's understandable why Nathan wouldn't want Doris to talk on the phone."

Maggie said with finality, "Tell the young lady to come and see me about the kitty auction, and we'll have a nice long talk."

When Qwilleran conveyed the invitation, he told Clarissa, "Maggie is from the moneyed families of Purple Point. Her great-grandmother owned a successful coal mine; she wore a long black dress with a little lace collar and carried a shotgun. Maggie prefers to live in the city and do humanitarian work. She's made it fashionable to volunteer at the animal shelter, and families now visit the shelter in their Sunday-best clothes on weekends, to see the cats and dogs, since we have no zoo. I warn you, Clarissa! Maggie has a very persuasive personality, and she doesn't even carry a shotgun."

:. The hot topic of conversation in coffee shops, at bridge clubs, and on the grapevine during late June was the Heirloom Auction—particularly the anonymity of donors.

The Lincoln copperplate in Tuesday's paper, the grandfather clock on Wednesday, the Victorian teacups on Thursday . . . who had donated them? Why the secrecy? The guesses and arguments that resulted constituted the best publicity the auction could have enjoyed!

Qwilleran knew the provenance of the three teacups, and he prepared to outbid any and all. He would give them to three women he knew.

Such was the suspense engendered by the Heirloom Auction series that tickets were sold out by Thursday night.

For Qwilleran, finding a subject for Friday's "Qwill Pen" was a problem. Clarissa's four-part series had said it all! The auction's charitable purpose, its organization and implementation, the enthusiasm of the student volunteers, and the generosity of the unnamed donors. Anything the "Qwill Pen" might say would be redundant, and yet readers would be disappointed if he overlooked the auction completely.

His solution: a nostalgic piece on the first auction he ever attended—and how he succeeded in outbidding an antique dealer for a historic rolltop desk. Purposely he neglected to mention the name of its famous, or infamous, owner—Ephraim Goodwinter. He knew the omission would bring a flood of mail from curious readers, keeping the office manager overworked for a week. Arch Riker would go into a rage over the "sly trick," although, Qwilleran knew, the editor in chief liked enthusiastic reader response.

When Qwilleran went to the paper to file his Friday copy, he passed the feature department and Clarissa caught his eye. She jumped up and joined him in the hallway. "Could we talk for a minute, Qwill?" She waved toward the empty conference room.

"I'll meet you there as soon as I throw my copy on Junior's desk."

"Aren't you a little late?"

"With malice aforethought," he explained. "When we're close to deadline, he doesn't have time to change anything. Editors like to edit."

In the managing editor's office, Junior grabbed the copy and rang for the copyboy. "Looks as if your girl's turning out all right, Qwill."

"She's not my girl. She applied for a job, and Arch hired her."

He joined Clarissa in the conference room.

In the empty room they sat at one corner of the long table.

"First let me compliment you on the auction series," he said. "You tackled the subject in depth without being stuffy."

"Thank you. It's my training. Did you have R and R when you were in J school?"

"It depends what you mean by those initials."

"Research and report. Each semester we were assigned a topic and had to explore it in depth and then write a report."

"What sort of topic?"

"Oh . . . the Volstead Act . . . the anatomy of cats . . . the naming of the original forty-eight states . . . mold as an environmental concern. The rule was: Collect all the available information—and then ask one more question."

"Did you have a favorite?"

"The naming of states was fun. Did you know that individuals react psychologically more strongly to state names beginning with a vowel than those beginning with a consonant? Texas is not only bigger than Ohio but has three strong consonants in the spelling."

"Hmmm. Under the circumstances, I'd say little Ohio has done quite well, despite all the vowels. Eight American presidents have come from Ohio, not to mention Thomas Edison and the Wright brothers." He could have mentioned Clark Gable, Doris Day, Cy Young, and Irma Bombeck, but Clarissa was rattling on.

"Are you from Ohio?" she asked.

"No, but the 'Qwill Pen' ran a series on nearby states called '*Know Your Neighbor*.'"

"I'd love to be a columnist," Clarissa said wistfully.

"Don't be too sure! A reporter gets an assignment and writes the necessary coverage, but a columnist always starts with nothing but a deep hole to fill."

Suddenly Arch Riker appeared in the doorway. "You two clear out! I'm having a meeting in this room."

"But I won't keep you, Qwill. I just wanted to give you some good news."

"You've had an offer from the *New York Times*."

With great joy she announced, "My best friend in California is coming for the Fourth of July weekend to attend the cat auction and bid on a kitten!"

"Good! Be sure to tell Maggie Sprenkle. It'll sound good in the publicity. Would he . . . or she . . . like to see *The Big Burning*? There are house seats available."

"She's my classmate from J school, but she went

into advertising. She also writes short stories and has sold a couple to crime magazines. She's hoping to find some juicy plot material while she's here."

He huffed into his moustache. He said, "Does your friend have a name? I hear the situation is so crowded on the West Coast, they're resorting to numbers."

On Friday night Qwilleran was sprawling in his lounge chair and reading to the Siamese. Yum Yum liked to sit on his lap and snuggle up to his ribs. The baritone vibrations reminded her, he had been told, of her mother's heartbeat while in the womb. Koko sat tall on the arm of the chair. Suddenly the phone rang, and Koko fell off. Yum Yum disappeared.

It was Polly, too excited to wait for his eleven o'clock call. "Qwill I have the most thrilling news! Orders are pouring in for the books you'll be signing next Wednesday. Already I've reordered twice."

"How do you account for that, Polly?"

"People tell me they're going to send books all over the country—to friends who grew up here and knew rumors of the enchanted castle in the woods. And Bushy's photos of the interiors will add to the excitement. Aren't you thrilled?"

Arrangements were made, sentiments were exchanged, and Qwilleran returned to his reading, only to be interrupted by the phone again.

"Qwill! I forgot to tell you the world-shaking news. Our crotchety mayor came into the store today and actually bought a book! What's more, she was congenial, according to the Green Smocks!"

"What did she buy?" he asked.

"You know it would be unethical to reveal customers' purchases," she said teasingly.

"You're just being rascally. Go back to your book. What are you reading?"

"That's privileged information."

And so it went.

It was the kind of bantering that always made Qwilleran's cats run around in circles. Why? Someday he would write a book. . . .

THIRTEEN

There was plenty to talk about that weekend—in the coffee shops, on the street corners, over the grapevine.

About the murder at the family reunion: "They've let the suspect go because of not-enough-evidence, but it looks like murder to me." ... "That's what happens when you have a lot of strangers coming into town." ... "Thank God it wasn't one of us."

About the new feature writer at the newspaper: "Why did they have to go to California to get somebody?" ... "Do you like the way she writes?"

About the Heirloom Auction: "Did you see that copper picture of Lincoln in the paper?" ... "My grandmother had a gold locket with Lincoln's picture on the front, his autograph on the back, and inside there was a smidgeon of cloth from the vest he was wearing when he was shot. The locket disappeared." ... "A lot of family treasures are coming out of the closet! They're not telling who-gives-what. Does it have something to do with income tax?"

About the *Big Burning* show: "You haven't seen it? I've seen it three times." ... "My great-grandparents lost their house, barns, livestock, everything! Lucky to escape with their kids."

About the weather: "Do you think this good weather will keep up?" ... "It's nice for parades and family reunions, but not so good for crops." ... "A good rain would wash the pollen away, too. Notice how many people are complaining about allergies?"

An editorial in Friday's paper was headlined:

CAMPBELL'S KIDS DO IT AGAIN

It praised the MCCC students of Burgess Campbell, who learned lifetime skills while contributing to the well-being of the community. Prodded by their mentor, they challenged a problem, devised an original solution, involved the General Public, and accomplished wonders. The General Public deserved much of the credit, but it was the enthusiasm of the young people that enlisted their support.

The editorial said: "There has never been an activity center for seniors. Burgess Campbell has donated an old downtown building; money to equip it is being raised by auctioning heirlooms donated by old families and collected by a crew of Kids. Local merchants, organizations, and news media are supporting it."

On Saturday morning auction-goers lined up in front of the Community Hall, waiting to buy tickets: five dollars for spectator seats in the balcony, twice that for persons intending to bid; they were given numbered flash cards.

Small objects were displayed on long tables lining the walls; large items were displayed on the platform. All had DO NOT TOUCH signs, and were under the watchful eye of security guards disguised as hosts and hostesses. There was even background music—not recorded but *live*: bouncy rhythms played by electric guitar, clarinet, and flute.

The emcee said, "Please take your seats: yellow tickets on the main floor, green tickets in the balcony."

There was a moment's hush, and then the chairman of the Kids extended a welcome and introduced Moose County's favorite auctioneer, "who is donating his expertise today, Foxy Fred." (Tumultuous applause!)

He entered wearing his usual outfit, which included sombrero, red neckerchief, and cowboy boots. "Howdy! Howdy!" he said. "As you good people know, there will be no noise of any kind while bidders are bidding and the porters and spotters are doing their job."

The porters and spotters and cashiers wore MCCC T-shirts, white on blue, with red neckerchiefs. All were emotionless, staring pointedly at the audience until there was an absolute hush.

Then a porter carried a framed picture to the

platform. Glancing at the tag, Foxy Fred said, "What we have here is an early-twentieth-century trolley car poster in mint condition, advertising a big bowl of healthy, crispy, crunchy breakfast cereal with strawberries and cream. What am I offered?"

"A hundred!" came a man's authoritative voice.

"A hundred I've got. Who'll make it two?"

"Two hundred!" came a voice that WPKX listeners recognized. There were gasps from the audience.

"Are you gonna let him get away with this rare piece of Americana?"

"Three!" shouted Qwilleran.

"Three I've got. Make it four . . ."

Wetherby flashed his card.

"Four I've got . . . Make it five? Make it five?"

The audience held its collective breath.

"Five I've got—from the man with a moustache! Now we're talkin'. . . . Make it six? Make it five-fifty . . . No? . . . Goin' at five hundred! Five hundred once, five hundred twice—"

Wetherby shouted, "Five-fifty!"

The audience roared.

"Six hundred!" Qwilleran shouted.

All eyes were on Wetherby, and he shook his head.

The audience groaned.

"Six hundred once, six hundred twice. Sold for a measly six hundred—this rare example of antiquity!"

The audience applauded as a spotter escorted Qwilleran to the nearest cashier.

Following the crowd-pleasing stunt, the auction settled down to reasonable bidding. Foxy Fred was a genius at manipulating an audience, and he coaxed the top dollar for the four items photographed for the newspaper, while letting other items move quickly. His technique added excitement and promised everyone a chance to take something home. If the bidding was slow, he shocked everyone by giving someone an incredible bargain. Or he mesmerized them with the auctioneer's chant: "Wanna wanna wanna wanna . . . bidda bidda bidda . . ."

There were short interludes for stretching legs and chattering, as well as long interludes for flocking to the lower level for cold drinks and sandwiches. Altogether he kept the crowd happy for six hours.

Polly said, "How does he maintain the pace?"

"He's a pro," Qwilleran said. "I'm waiting to see how he handles the cat auction next Saturday."

The Lincoln portrait went for four thousand, the tall case clock for three thousand, and the three porcelain teacups to Qwilleran for three hundred.

Polly gasped, "Qwill, what are you going to do with them?"

"Give tea parties," he said glibly.

It was an anonymous donation that caused the greatest stir. It had been the last of the important items photographed in the *Something*—a massive library table of carved oak, with two bulbous legs at one end and a realistic carving of a basset hound standing on hind legs and supporting the table at the other end. It had belonged to the affluent father of Sarah Plensdorf, according to people in the know. Whispered comments were: "Bet she's glad to get rid of it." ... "Who on earth would want such a monster?" ... "How much do you think they'll pay?"

A sealed bid from an agent in Lockmaster— unchallenged—won the table for ten thousand!

. . .

When Qwilleran and Polly left the auction scene, he had his teacups and she had an autographed copy of Mark Twain's travel book *A Tramp Abroad*. She said, "It will please Lisa Compton that I bought the book; it belonged to her great-grandmother, who had the thrill of meeting Mark Twain when he lectured here in 1895. . . . Just think, Qwill, he spoke in the old opera house—the very stage where you do *The Big Burning*. It gives me goose bumps!"

"Where would your goose bumps like to have dinner?" he asked. "How about the Boulder House Inn—far from the bidding crowd?"

"I think it would be lovely," Polly said, ignoring his pun.

Before driving to the lakeshore, they stopped at the barn to feed the cats. Polly's cats had an automatic feeder that could be set for any hour, but Koko let it be known that he disapproved of automation.

From the barn Qwilleran phoned the inn for a reservation, and they drove leisurely through the countryside.

Polly said, "Everyone's talking about the ten-thousand-dollar bid from Lockmaster—for the

Plensdorf library table. Can you think of anyone down there who would pay that?"

"Some sharpie who'll sell it for twenty thousand in Chicago. When they send a truck to pick it up, we should have our spies follow it."

She could not be sure whether he was serious or tossing one of his flip remarks. Rather than reveal her naïveté, she remained silent.

Qwilleran said, "This is the third time I've seen Foxy Fred in action. Do you think he will use the same sharp, scolding, bossy tactics with an audience of cat lovers? I should think the right approach would be gentler, appealing to their sentimentality. Also, I can't visualize the platform procedure of a cat auction."

"Well, you remember Peggy, who comes to the store twice a day to feed Dundee, don't you, Qwill? She's been volunteering at the animal shelter. She says each cat will arrive onstage in his own 'limousine'—a picnic basket with lift-up lid and top-handle. His name and other information will be on a tag attached to the handle. And the tags are being hand-lettered and decorated by art students. There's a soft pad in the bottom of each basket.

Each cat is spending a few hours each day in his own private limousine to familiarize himself with the aroma."

Qwilleran said, "The well-organized routine sounds as if Hixie Rice has had a hand in the planning," he said with a touch of sarcasm, for which Polly rebuked him.

It was generally thought that Hixie's brilliant plans always went awry. Thus far, her plans for *Pickax Now* had been successful. Even the weather had cooperated, and the three-month celebration was almost two-thirds over. Still, Qwilleran could not quell the newsman's suspicion that everything was going too well.

FOURTEEN

🐾 Hixie Rice was flying high! Sell-out audiences were having a good cry at *The Big Burning* and laughing in all the right places at *Billy the Kid*. Family reunions were a success—with one exception, the shooting. Who really killed the rabbit hunter?

Everyone was looking forward to the second parade.

One day Qwilleran entered the following in his journal:

———————————

Today the cats and I were enjoying the gazebo when Culvert McBee came walking up the lane carrying a plastic sack. His mother makes the best chocolate chip cookies in the county! And I was prepared with a limerick:

> *Fresh cookies from Mrs. McBee*
> *Are always received with glee!*
> *Does she bake each batch*
> *Of cookies from scratch?*
> *Or do they grow on a tree?*

How that boy has grown! I remember him when he was a nine-year-old defeating adults in a spelling bee! Since then his parents have encouraged him in a series of worthwhile enterprises, including a backyard shelter for old, sick, abandoned dogs.

I invited him to sit down, but he said he had to go home and do chores. Yet he showed a certain heel-kicking reluctance to leave.

"Is something on your mind?" I asked him.

He said the new girl at the paper found out

about his backyard shelter and wants to write about it. His father said no, explaining that people all over the county will be dumping the unwanted dogs on the McBee farm.

I told Culvert his father is absolutely right! I said I would explain it to the new girl.

Only yesterday she informed me the cat club had invited her to join it, and enter Jerome in the cat fashion show. He had won one in California.

I pointed out to her that she was brought here as a journalist to report on such events—not as a joiner of organizations seeking publicity.

Qwilleran was looking forward to another book signing on Wednesday. The Literary Club was introducing *The Historic Hibbard House*: text by James Mackintosh Qwilleran and photographs by John Bushland.

All the best people assembled on the lower floor of The Pirate's Chest.

They rose to their feet in a vociferous welcome when the author stepped to the podium and the photographer projected the first image in the darkened room. It was the century-old mansion of eccentric design and curious legend—that had been reduced to ashes overnight.

Bushland's photo of the strange architecture made a striking illustration for the dust jacket of *The Historic Hibbard House*. Stranger still was the color of the jacket—a flowery shade of violet. Qwilleran explained it to the audience:

"Four generations occupied this house. It was built by a wealthy sawmill owner who could neither read nor write. . . . His son, college-bred, lived his life as a country gentlemen who liked to entertain guests. . . . His grandson was a serious scholar, noted for his library. . . . His great-granddaughter and last of the Hibbards was a professor of drama and poetry. Her name was Violet."

🐾 The morning after the book signing, Qwilleran walked downtown to Lanspeak's Department Store to buy a violet-scented gift for Polly, who had originally suggested the color of the book jacket.

Carol Lanspeak was at the cosmetics counter, arranging a display. "Can you believe it? We're having a run on violet this morning! I'm going to do a window on the color—with items from all over the store, and with books courtesy of The Pirate's Chest."

For Polly, Carol suggested a light violet scent in a gold filigree bottle. "Do you have time to go back to the office and say hello to Larry?"

The owner of the store was frowning over record books. "Come in! Come in! Have a cup of coffee, I'm ready to take a break."

"I saw you and Carol at the meeting last night."

"Compliments on a good presentation. Carol and I knew the Hibbards."

"I suppose you know the Ledfields," Qwilleran said.

"Quite well, although they don't socialize like the other old-timers. Our daughter is their physician."

"Is that so?" Qwilleran sensed another link in the Ledfield Saga.

The Lanspeaks were fine old stock like the Ledfields but chose to live in a rambling farmhouse in the hills and join in the business life and community interests of the county. Their daughter was a physician practicing locally and living in Indian Village.

Suddenly Carol breezed into the office saying in a low voice, "Larry, strangers in jewelry. Would you see what they're all about?"

Larry dashed out, and Qwilleran asked, "Are you having any trouble this summer?"

"We're seeing a lot of new faces," she said, "but there are strangers—and *strangers*! When Larry and I were in New York, trying to get into theatre, we both worked as store detectives—and learned plenty! This year our six-foot-two stockboy from Wildcat has been promoted to store detective, but this is his day off."

"Is he a Cuttlebrink?" Qwilleran asked, exhibiting his local savvy.

"Aren't they all?" She rolled her eyes.

She said, "You were asking about the Ledfields. They go to our church, and twenty years ago the Sunday school had a hands-on program for youngsters. Each child adopted a lonely widow or a couple who were childless. They sent handmade greeting cards throughout the year to their 'adopted' elders—"

"Great idea!" Qwilleran said. "Is the program still going?"

"I'm afraid not," Carol said. "It was the pet project of Agatha Burns, one of your '*Late Greats*.'

"But one of the Happy Endings is that Diane has grown up and become a physician and has 'adopted' Doris and Nathan, who enjoy the luxury of receiving house calls."

"Beautiful story," Qwilleran said.

🐾 Following the visit with Carol and Larry, Qwilleran wrote a note to their daughter, drove to Indian Village, and dropped it in her mailbox:

Thursday

Dear Diane,

Were your ears burning this morning? Your parents were telling me about Agatha Burns's idea for Sunday school—and how your adopted "aunt" became a lifelong friend.

The reason I'm writing: A mutual friend has been trying to get in touch with Doris and is told repeatedly that she is unwell. She's concerned.

Qwill

In early evening, Diane phoned. "I know you're busy, and I appreciate your taking the time to notify me. I checked her condition this afternoon and found it wise to consult an allergy specialist in Lockmaster. We both think we should have an environmental investigation. Those old houses are terribly damp. Thank you for the tip."

When Qwilleran phoned Polly at eleven o'clock, she was effervescing with news. "Clarissa returned Doris's diamond ring, as you suggested, and today Doris sent it back to Clarissa with a touching note. It said, 'I think of you as the daughter I never had!' Clarissa is keeping the ring in a safety box at the bank, but first she had it appraised by a jeweler in Lockmaster."

"Did she say what it's worth?"

"No. And I didn't ask, dear!" Polly said archly.

"I admire your restraint," he replied, equally arch.

Having enjoyed that bit of badinage, they settled down to their usual exchange of news.

"Wetherby's giving a pizza party for Clarissa's guest," Polly said.

"That comes as no surprise," replied Qwilleran.

"Do you want to go to the cat auction, Qwill?"

"It's one event I can afford to skip, although I'm curious to know how Foxy Fred is going to handle those kittens without terrifying them."

"Peggy says it's going to be filmed."

"Good! Sign me up for two videos."

"Well, *à bientôt*, dear."

"À bientôt!"

Before he could call "treat" to the cats, the phone rang again. Obviously, Polly had an afterthought. He picked it up.

"On second thought, I'll take three videos," he said.

"*What? What?* . . . Qwill. Is this Qwill?" came a distraught voice. It was Maggie Sprenkle.

"Sorry. I thought it was someone else. Is this Maggie? What's wrong. This is Qwill."

"Oh, Qwill! Have you heard the bad news?" Panic was added to the aging voice.

"No! What's the trouble?"

"There's been a terrible accident! Foxy Fred fell out of a tree. His back is broken." She stopped to wail in anguish!

Qwilleran was silent with shock and what it would mean.

"Did you hear me, Qwill?"

"This is terrible! What was he doing in the tree?"

"Cutting off a branch that had tent worms, they say. Lost his footing on the ladder."

"What will this do to the auction plans?" After he had said it, he knew it was a stupid question.

"You'll have to come to the rescue, Qwill! You're the only one who can do it. People are coming from all over the state. TV crews, too."

"What can I say, Maggie? Will you let me think about it?"

"You can't! You can't! No one else can do it!" She was still sobbing, and he began to worry about her having a stroke.

"All right. All right. Calm down, Maggie. Have a cup of tea, and don't worry about a thing. I'll do it. We'll talk about it in the morning. No problem. . . . Do you hear?"

Stunned, he returned to the kitchen to give the cats a treat, then conducted them wordlessly to their sleeping quarters on the third level and watched them hop into their respective baskets. Their door was left open, so they could roam during the night, observing who-knows-what feline rituals. Qwilleran always closed his own door.

On this occasion he retired fearing he would not sleep, and he was right. He had entertained doubts about the kitty auction when it was Foxy Fred's responsibility; now he envisioned a new problem. The kittens had been rehearsing, but not in a strange building before a large—and probably overexcited—audience.

One o'clock. Two o'clock. At two-thirty he became aware of a scratching at his door and a rattling of his door handle.

He jumped out of bed, and there they were—a couple of cool cats. Koko looked around as if saying, "Here we are!"

"You rascals!" Qwilleran said, as he sprawled in his thinking chair. The cats joined him—Yum Yum cozily on his lap and Koko on the arm of the chair, from which he stared at the man's forehead. A calm invaded the room. Qwilleran thought, Anyone who can play the lead in *King Lear* at the age of fifteen and direct a high school production of *Life with Father* at the age of sixteen should be able to handle a cat auction. . . . Think of it as showbiz . . . with a cast of forty scene stealers! . . . An audience of cat lovers will be a pushover! . . . We'll not only get their money, we'll show them a good time!

He shooed the cats out of the room and went to bed.

"Wanna wanna wanna wanna . . . bidda bidda bidda bidda."

He mesmerized himself to sleep.

FIFTEEN

The Siamese sensed something was queer on Friday morning. Their breakfast had been served at seven A.M., and his and her plates had been accidentally reversed under the kitchen table.

As for Qwilleran, he was having a Continental breakfast at the animal shelter with the two chairpersons of the kitty auction, both of them residents of Winston Park. Peggy Marsh was the young computer programmer who went to The Pirate's Chest twice a day to feed Dundee and "tidy up" his private domain. Judd Amhurst was the retiree who divided his time between the bookstore (managing special events) and the animal shelter (bathing the scruffy abandoned dogs brought to the shelter by rescue officers).

At the shelter the forty kittens occupied group cages but were transferred to their personal "limousines" for the rehearsal. One by one Qwilleran lifted them out of their baskets for fondling and sweet talk. They were hypnotized by the resonance of his voice and fascinated by his moustache.

Peggy said, "At the community hall tomorrow there'll be an audience of hundreds, according to the advance ticket sales, but the kittens will be mildly sedated."

"The main problem," said Qwilleran, remembering Koko's disastrous stage debut, "will be to keep the audience from shouting and screaming."

Judd said they could arrange to print some signs in a hurry: QUIET! KITTENS ASLEEP! "They could have an artist do some sketches of them; folks could take them home for a donation."

The rehearsal ended with coffee and sweet rolls from Lois's Luncheonette.

Judd said, "Did you know that her son is starting a lunchwagon, to be parked at special events? It'll be in the parking lot tomorrow."

Peggy said, "We're printing souvenir programs for the auction, listing kittens' formal names, nick-names, and markings."

Finally, Judd said, "If this auction is a success, we'll try one with puppies, and I'd buy one if they permitted dogs at Winston Park."

Qwilleran said, "Why not take the plunge to-morrow, Judd? I was a dog man myself until I came under the spell of you-know-who."

You-know-who were waiting on Qwilleran with what he considered a lack of enthusiasm. He took a shower and put his clothes in the washer. His housemates still greeted him as if his morning had been spent in illegal or immoral activity.

He gave them a treat. He brushed their coats. He read to them about bug and bird voices in Hawthorne's book, then toted them to the gazebo to experience bugs and birds firsthand. For himself he took the cell phone and some chocolate chip cookies.

All three of them seemed to feel a strangeness in the atmosphere. Everything was still, as if waiting for something. The sky, though sunny, was a sick yellow.

Then the phone calls started.

Clarissa called to say that her friend Vicki was arriving in late afternoon and was excited about adopting a kitten but would be unable to stay for Monday's parade because she was starting a new job on Tuesday at an important ad agency.

Qwilleran commented, "For anyone who has seen the Tournament of Roses in California, the Tournament of Peonies in Pickax will be no great loss."

Then Polly called praising Qwilleran for his noble offer to handle the auction and regretting that she could not attend; she had to work. She mentioned that Dundee had been acting freakish all day, as if he sensed a change in the weather.

In late afternoon Wetherby Goode phoned, saying in glum tones, "They're gonna shoot the weatherman for sure when they hear the six P.M. forecast."

Qwilleran said, "Better come here for a nip before you go to the station, Joe—since you predict this may be the last we'll ever hear."

He carried everyone and everything indoors to hear the bad news.

"The sad truth is this," said the meteorologist when he was seated at the bar with a drink and a bowl of mixed nuts. "That storm front that's been stalled over Canada all summer is starting to move over the lakes. It should hit here Sunday. High winds, torrential rain! What they call a Northern Hurricane. You might as well cancel *The Big Burning*. People won't want to drive. The rain comes in sheets. We can expect power outages. Does this barn have a generator? If not, better move back to the Village temporarily. We're equipped to take care of blackouts. And our streets are paved."

Qwilleran said, "I hope your weathercast tonight isn't going to scare the public away from my auction tomorrow."

"No, it's intended to give them time to stock up on flashlight batteries, canned soup, and cat and dog food."

. . .

On Saturday morning, the Forty Famous Felines were being transported in their group cages to the community hall, where they were given a light repast with a little something added to make them feel good about their adventure. The volunteers who attended them were accustomed to speaking in soothing voices, and they would transfer each kitten to his limousine in the proper order. A few salty tears would be shed over kittens like Prince Hal, Lorna Doone, and Rum Tum Tugger, who were going out into the wide world.

From the waiting room on the lower level, each limousine would be brought to the stage, carried by MCCC spotters, trained for the assignment. The bleak stage was made friendly by a few potted plants lent by florists, and the auctioneer's table in center front was softened with a paisley shawl lent by Maggie Sprenkle herself. Qwilleran was wearing his silk shirt in a neutral color that would show the kittens' markings to advantage. Purposely, his moustache had not been trimmed.

As the excited audience began to gather, spotters pointed to signs saying: QUIET! KITTENS ASLEEP!

Four-page catalogs were handed out, listing twenty males and twenty females by their glamorous names, their nicknames, along with markings and eye color.

When the seats were filled on the main floor and balcony, the main doors were closed, and the welcome was made by Maggie Sprenkle, an important figure in the local aristocracy as well as animal welfare.

She said, "We know you're going to adore these kitties and want to scream in delight, but—please keep your voices to a low murmur. And when our auctioneer makes his bow don't welcome him with thunderous applause, but . . . remember the kitties!"

When Qwilleran made his entrance, the enthusiasm threatened to explode. Here was Mr. Q in person! But he held up both hands for silence, and proceeded to thrill them with the depth and warmth of his mellifluous voice.

"Friends, let's review the rules of the game. All of you who have bought bidding tickets have also received numbered flash cards. There will be no shouting of bids. Flash cards will be used to make bids in silence. . . . Let me see your flash cards!" A flutter of numbers filled the main hall.

The eight spotters were women students in MCCC T-shirts, and their delight in this assignment was reflected in their happy faces. Those in the aisles would watch for the flashing of cards when the auctioneer said, "Who'll give me three hundred?" The spotters would point and say, "Hep!" When the top bid was reached, the spotter would return the lucky kitten to his limousine and escort the winning bidder and his purchase to the cashier in the lobby. The spotters also warned noisy members of the audience, and the auctioneer would halt the bidding until the disturbance ended.

When the first limousine was brought to the paisley-draped table, Qwilleran read the name tag and said, "We are starting with a member of royalty: Princess Isabella! [General murmur.] She is a white calico with soft gray markings and a distinctive personality. She knows she'll grow up to be a queen, and she's going to have fun while she can." [Wriggle of anticipation in the audience.] Qwilleran opened the lid of the basket slowly and peeked inside, then lifted the kitten gently. [Excited murmur.] Isabella raised her head and looked at the audience with golden eyes.

"Aw-w-w!" came a murmur from the hall.

Qwilleran said, "We're told she has a playful disposition in spite of her royal antecedents." He shifted his grip on her, and she looked at his hand then opened her pink mouth and rested her sharp little teeth on his finger.

"Aw-w-w!" was the sentimental murmur, louder this time, and the spotters in the aisles held up warning hands.

The auctioneer said, "Shall we start with . . . five hundred?" A flutter of flash cards led him to raise the bid to seven . . . then eight-fifty . . . finally a thousand.

"A thousand, I've got! A thousand once . . . a thousand twice . . . Sold to number ninety-three!"

A spotter led two young women from their seats, and another took Isabella in her limousine to meet them. As they went up the aisle to the cashier, Qwilleran realized that one of them was Clarissa

Moore. Her tanned, well-groomed companion, who had just bought Isabella, must be her friend Vicki.

There were no more thousand-dollar bids that morning but it telegraphed the message that a thousand is not too much to pay for a kitten. Bids didn't go that high again until late afternoon but anything less than five hundred seemed an affront to a Puck, or an Iago or a Cleopatra.

No other kitten bit the auctioneer's finger, but several reached up and touched his moustache with a trembling paw, at which the audience murmured, "Aw-w-w!"

After twenty kittens had been adopted, there was an intermission, when bidders could eat a picnic lunch on the lower level or buy one from Lois's Lunchwagon in the parking lot. Backstage everyone was complimenting everyone else, and when the afternoon session opened, Qwilleran complimented the holders of flash cards for their cooperation.

He conducted swift transactions. If the bidding

dragged, he removed the subject from the block, rather than insult a personage of such importance as: Nanki-Poo, Mary Poppins, or Jane Austen.

Toward the end of the afternoon there was one more high-dollar bid. The kitten was a reddish brown male with a cocky manner and a swaggering walk. "A man's cat," the volunteers had written on his name tag.

When his turn came at the auction table, Qwilleran looked at the name tag and said to the audience, "'If you can keep your head when all about you are losing theirs . . .' This is Rudyard Kipling, who also answers to the name of Rudy!"

He lifted the muscular kitten from the limousine, and there was an appreciative murmur through the audience.

"To start, who'll give me five hundred? [Several cards flashed.] Who'll give me seven hundred? . . . Make it eight . . . Make it eight! . . . Eight I've got. Make it nine! Make it a thousand."

Only one card flashed. "Hep!" said the spotter.

Qwilleran saw the white hair. It was Judd Amhurst bidding the high dollar! He must be buying it for one of his married sons out west.

Backstage the volunteers were ecstatic about the outcome of the auction, and Maggie Sprenkle clasped Qwilleran's hand in both of hers.

"We realized over twenty thousand dollars for the shelter! How can we thank you, Qwill, for your tremendous contribution?"

"The experience is all the reward I need," he assured her.

On the way home Qwilleran stopped at the bookstore.

Polly said, "Clarissa brought her friend into the store today to show me Isabella, the kitten she bought. Is it a fact that the top bid was a thousand? Amazing."

"Isn't it? Remember that the K Fund will match it. Wait till Bart hears about it! It won't surprise him. Attorneys are surprise proof. I think it's an oath they take when they're admitted to the Bar. Judd bought Rudyard Kipling for the same amount—for one of his sons, no doubt."

"No, Qwill! Rudyard Kipling is for himself! He says he couldn't resist the sales pitch, and he liked the idea of getting a literary cat."

Polly said, "Now about Vicki. She's not staying

as long as she planned. She starts a new job Tuesday morning, and she wants to get home to help her kitten adjust and prepare herself for a new work challenge. So she'll have to miss *The Big Burning* and Monday's parade."

Polly said, "Vicki was sorry she couldn't stay to meet you, Qwill, but she left a note for you."

It was an unusual shade of gray, with her monogram in white on the envelope flap. It was apparently something she had written before leaving home. He slipped it into his coat pocket.

Late Saturday evening, as Qwilleran was considering a bedtime read for the cats, Koko was more interested in the kitchen window than the bookshelf. He kept jumping on the kitchen counter and staring at the blackness outdoors.

"Expecting someone?" he asked. Then he realized how long it had been since Andrew Brodie had dropped in for a nightcap. He phoned the police chief at home, and in five minutes the big burly Scot was barging into the kitchen demanding, "Where's my smart cat? Where's my little sweetheart?" He dropped on a stool at the snack bar where Qwilleran had prepared a tray of Scotch, ice cubes, and cheese.

The Siamese frisked about, happy to see him: Andy usually maneuvered a few crumbs of cheese to them.

To Qwilleran he said, "Been listening to Joe on the air. That storm that's been stalled over Canada has started moving across the lakes. It might reach us by tomorrow and eliminate our parade on Monday."

"We can hardly complain," Qwilleran said. "We've had a spectacularly good summer."

"It's a pity, though. Our granddaughter is supposed to be on the Queen's float, and my wife is cutting a truckload of peonies in our backyard for the parade."

"Joe has been wrong before, Andy."

"Yeah, but . . . What kind of cheese is this? It's good!"

"It's domestic. Not all the good stuff comes from Switzerland and France. How's everything at City Hall, Andy? Who's watering the pansies?"

"Ach, mon! We haven't had trouble with the vandals all summer."

"Do you know that woman in Kennebeck who sees into the future, Andy?"

"She goes to our church. A fine woman. She saw the shooting as a crime, not an accident, but that doesn't hold up in court."

Qwilleran could have told him about Koko's death howl, signifying foul play, but as evidence it lacked credibility, to say the least.

Suddenly Koko emerged from somewhere and hopped up to the kitchen window, where he stared out with ears alert and tail pointed.

Both men turned to look at the dark glass.

In a minute or two, they heard a muffled blast and saw a bright flash in the dark sky.

Brodie jumped to his feet, talked on his cell phone, hurried to the door. "Crazies! Firebombed the window boxes at city hall!"

He rushed to his vehicle leaving Qwilleran to reflect: the anti-pansy faction! . . . Too bad. Another idea of Hixie's ruined but she won't give up!

Only then did it dawn on Qwilleran that Koko had been staring out the window into the blackness for half an hour—before the blast.

That cat! Qwilleran thought. He looks like a cat,

walks like a cat, talks like a cat, but he knows what's going to happen—like that woman in Kennebeck. Is it because he has sixty whiskers instead of the normal forty-eight?

Baffled, he scooped himself a dish of ice cream.

SIXTEEN

Early Sunday morning, two surprised Siamese were stuffed into their cat carrier and loaded into the SUV along with luggage, a food cooler, "Qwill Pen" notes, and desk clutter. Qwilleran had brought the outdoor furniture in from the gazebo and stacked it in the foyer, and Pat O'Dell's maintenance crew would disassemble the gazebo screens and otherwise storm proof the barn for a short absence.

They were moving to their condo in Indian Village, which was in a strip of four, called the Willows and shared with Polly, Wetherby Goode, and Dr. Connie, the veterinarian.

When the refugees from the barn arrived, the village management had already shuttered the large glass window walls and sandbagged the banks of the creek that they overlooked.

Eliminating the view made for a gloomy interior, but Qwilleran could read and the cats could sleep and Wetherby would find excuses for parties.

This would be the first time the connecting doors between the underground garages had ever been used.

Qwilleran notified Wetherby when he arrived. Then they joined Dr. Connie and Polly at the weatherman's unit for an impromptu lunch.

As they waited for the wind and rain to strike, conversation about the weather was avoided.

Polly talked about the success of the "violet" book. Qwilleran said he'd like to write a biography of the late Homer Tibbitt. Connie talked about her new marmalade cat, a litter mate of Dundee. The host played the piano.

Then the wind came up, and it started to rain

hard, and they returned to their respective condos—through the basement tunnel—to be with their pets, who would need comforting. The question of who-comforted-whom was a topic for Qwilleran to cover in his journal that night. He wrote:

Sunday—I daresay no one is sleeping tonight, least of all Koko and Yum Yum. The wind screeches; the rain slaps against the building. It stops for a while, and the cats crawl out from under the blankets, and then it starts again, with renewed ferocity.

During the lulls, Joe calls all of us to see if we're okay. He warns us that it may start again.

And it does!

I'm no radio-nut myself, but everyone else in the county tunes in WPKX newbites, especially on weekends and holidays, when the *Something* doesn't publish. The station calls their newsbites a public service, but I suspect they're just trying to scoop the newspaper. Furthermore, why should I listen to the newsbites, when all my friends are addicted and will phone me with the news of the latest fires, thefts, accidents, and other calamities?

It's the Moose County Grapevine.

All night a howling, blasting wind and a drenching, whipping rain took turns in tormenting the residents of the Willows. No one could get any sleep, least of all the six cats.

On Monday, the second day of the sporadic hurricane, Junior Goodwinter, the managing editor of the paper, called.

"The way it looks, no paper tomorrow, but a skeleton crew is on call, and we might put out a Hurricane Edition—just a few pages with emergency news. We see it as a collector's item, a sort of historical document."

"Is there anything I can do, Junior?"

"You might write a short 'Qwill Pen' piece about Cool Koko's reaction to the hurricane—something to make readers smile."

Judd Amhurst called from Winston Park. "Lucky to be out there, Qwill. Will you tell Polly that we rescued Dundee from the bookstore, and he's staying with Peggy? Rudy is with me, keeping his head while all the rest of us are losing ours."

Hixie Rice called. "Glad you made it back to the condo, Qwill. Most of us are sitting it out at the clubhouse." (He thought, Getting sloshed.)

He said, "Too bad about the parade."

Then Polly called to remark that the wind had quieted a little. Qwilleran told her the good news about Dundee.

"Wait a minute! There's a death notice on the radio!" In a minute she returned. "Doris Ledfield died tonight! Following a respiratory infection! I'll hang up in case they broadcast more details."

Before she could call back, Maggie Sprenkle phoned.

"Qwill, I feel awful! I was so elated yesterday after the auction, and now I feel terrible! First I heard about dear Doris's passing on the radio, and I couldn't believe it! No one knew she was that ill! But when I called the Old Manse to talk to Nathan, the nurse said he was quite ill himself and couldn't speak to anyone!" She stopped to sob. "Perhaps I shouldn't tell you this, Qwill, but I must talk to someone!"

"I understand, Maggie," he said. "Consider me a member of the family."

After a few more tears she felt the strength to go on.

"We were very close—the Sprenkles and the Ledfields—and Nathan once told Jeremy and me in our rose garden, when Doris was having one of her setbacks, that he couldn't live without her. And if anything happened to her, life would have no meaning. He could not go on alone.

"We mumbled words of sympathy and affection, but I have always been haunted by that recollection. I can't help wondering if he'll do something rash. . . ." She burst into tears again.

"It's understandable, Maggie. It was right to share it with me. Have a cup of tea, and remember what Jeremy would say."

"You're right, Qwill. Thank you so much." As she hung up, he could hear one more painful wail.

Koko had been listening, and he rushed around growling before throwing back his head and uttering what Qwilleran had come to know as his death howl.

Before the night was over, Qwilleran's phone rang frequently, as friends felt it their duty to keep him informed:

"The Road Commission is telling drivers to stay off the highway, Qwill."

"The worst is the Bloody Creek Bridge."

"The commission has been promising to fix that deathtrap for years. They've had five accidents; how many do they have to have before they act? What am I paying my taxes for?"

That was Junior Goodwinter.

Qwilleran's phone rang repeatedly. Everyone wanted to talk. He had a feeling of foreboding. Even the cats were edgy.

Later Wetherby called.

"Did you hear about the accident at Bloody Creek Bridge? Name withheld. I called the Station, and one of my buddies told me the name of the driver . . . Liz Hart!"

"Where was Derek?"

"They drive separate cars; they work different hours. After working late as maître d', he'll sometimes bunk on a cot at the restaurant so he can do early shopping for groceries the next morning."

"What was she doing on the Bloody Creek Bridge? That's north of here?" Qwilleran asked.

"Interesting question."

"Did the newsbite tell whether the car was traveling north or south?"

"They never give details."

Qwilleran speculated, "If she was northbound, she was going to the Lanspeaks. They live in the Hummocks, and they've been like godparents to both Liz and Derek. And Diane Lanspeak is probably Liz's doctor. . . . If we don't hear any further details, I suppose we could check with them, Joe."

"Liz would want you to know, Qwill. She says you saved her life on Grand Island and were responsible for her coming to Moose County and meeting Derek Cuttlebrink. I understand she comes from a very wealthy family in Chicago, but she was glad to get away from them. Fortunately, she had money from her deceased father."

"Is that so?" Qwilleran murmured, although he knew more than Wetherby did. "Liz gave me an antique chair that belonged to her father. Sitting in it is supposed to improve your intelligence."

"I should borrow it," Wetherby said. "Does it sound as if the wind is picking up again? I'd better go and hold Jet Stream's paw."

SEVENTEEN

After a bad night, Qwilleran prepared breakfast for two nervous cats. They huddled side by side with their legs tucked under their bodies.

As Qwilleran prepared their food, he entertained them with a few observations from Jerome K. Jerome, whose needs were satisfied with a homely home, small pleasures, one or two friends, a pipe to smoke, a cat, a dog, enough to eat, and enough to drink.

The Siamese regarded each other questioningly.

Then Koko bit Yum Yum gently on the back of the neck. She liked it.

Next the phone rang. This time it was Clarissa. "Qwill, have you heard the news on WPKX? Doris Ledfield has died! I had no idea she was so ill! I feel I should do something, but I don't know what."

Qwilleran felt uncomfortable himself but could think of nothing comforting to say. "Maggie Sprenkle was Doris's closest friend," he said, "and she's a total wreck. Perhaps you could call her and commiserate. It might help you both."

They hung up, and almost immediately Clarissa called again. "I forgot to tell you, Qwill, Vicki called from California this morning. Isabella slept on her pillow. She loves that kitten! Vicki was sorry she didn't meet you, Qwill. She left a note for Polly to give you."

Qwilleran thought, Note . . . note . . . where is it? To Clarissa he said, "I'll drop Vicki a line as soon as the turmoil subsides."

After Clarissa's call, he began to wonder about that note. He had put it in his coat pocket at the bookstore. It was probably hanging in his closet. It was still at the barn and would remain there for a while.

He was sitting at the dining table that served as a desk at the condo. His papers were there. His phone was there. His old typewriter was there. His copier was there. And suddenly Koko was there, scattering desk clutter.

"Down!" he shouted, and Koko dashed out of sight.

That smart cat had made his point! Among the papers was Vicki's letter. It had not been left in his coat pocket. He added it to a stack of things-to-do.

Tuesday was his usual day for transacting K Fund business with the attorney. He phoned Bart at home.

There followed the predictable weather talk:

"How's the weather out there?" Qwilleran asked. "And how bad are the roads?"

"Not bad. The creek's running a little high, and everyone's disappointed about the parade. My kids were to be on one of the floats and so were my wife's prize peonies. . . . Are you printing a paper tomorrow?"

"We plan to. Can you get here for our regular meeting? I'm at the condo, not the barn."

"Be there at ten-thirty. I suppose you heard the bad news about Nathan Ledfield's wife?"

"Too bad. I never met her, but I hear she was charming."

"Yes, and my wife says she played the piano like an angel! When she accompanied Nathan on the violin, it was . . . what shall I say? . . . too good for Moose County. (Don't quote me.) Enough of this chitchat. I sound as if I have cabin fever. I probably do. Look forward to seeing you tomorrow."

As Qwilleran turned away from the phone, he caught Koko disarranging the stack of mail to be answered, and the cat was particularly interested in the unusual gray envelope with white monogram. In fact, there were fang marks in one corner.

"What do you think you're doing," Qwilleran demanded in a sharp tone that sent Koko flying to parts unknown.

It was possible that Vicki used scented writing paper, but a sniff dispelled that notion.

Still, Qwilleran's curiosity was aroused. His ruminations were interrupted by an excited phone call. It was from Larry Lanspeak.

"Qwill, I've got some bad news about our daughter's two patients in Purple Point! She's lost Doris and Nathan. Same diagnosis—respiratory complications! It's that moldy old mansion they've always lived in! I don't mean to be heartless. Diane's associate in Lockmaster ordered an environmental investigation. Don't know whether they got around to it. Everyone's too busy these days! Well, thought you'd want to know."

Qwilleran hung up the phone slowly as he thought of this wealthy couple with so many worldly goods and so much musical talent and so much love for each other—disappointed because they had no children.

Unexpectedly Koko landed in his lap and stared at him belligerently.

He wants me to do something, Qwilleran thought. His eyes strayed across the desk to Vicki's letter. He opened the envelope and read the computer-printed letter quickly, then he read it a second time and phoned the attorney.

"Bart! I've discovered a document that you should see as soon as possible! It's imperative that you come down this afternoon!"

. . .

When the attorney arrived, Qwilleran's first words were: "I just heard the bad news about Nathan Ledfield."

"Yes, their housekeeper called me after you and I talked. It's an end of an era! . . . What's the document you mentioned?"

"Sit down first, and let me pour you a cup of coffee."

When that was done, Qwilleran said, "To put it bluntly, I have a strong suspicion the Ledfields were murdered."

Bart all but choked on the coffee. "Is this a theory of yours? Or do you have evidence?"

"I received a letter from a friend of Clarissa Moore, our new feature writer at the *Something*. The women were friends in California. The writer of the letter made a flying trip here this past weekend for the purpose—believe it or not—of buying a kitten in the auction at the animal shelter on Saturday."

Barter said, "Which you conducted with spectacular success, I'm told."

Qwilleran nodded modestly and said, "I didn't meet the young lady, but she left a note for me, which I'd like you to read."

The letter, on gray stationery, read as follows:

Dear Qwill,

Sorry not to meet you. Clarissa has told me so much about you. . . . Don't tell her about this note. You'll see why. She and I used to double-date on ski weekends with Harvey Ledfield and my friend Greg. We always had a lot to talk about. I was taking a correspondence course in mystery writing; every murder mystery has to have Motive, Opportunity, and Method. And I told them how the hardest part is finding an un-usual method. You can't have the butler poison-ing the soup anymore.

Clarissa, who had been doing research on mold for a school assignment, said that mold found in old houses could cause illness—or even death in old people—and maybe I could use it in a story. Greg, who was in the building business, said the mold, a fungus, could be implanted in the air ducts of a building.

I said I would try using it in a story, and if it sold, I would split the commission with them. (I wrote it, but it didn't sell.)

I said I'd have to go back to poison in the soup. Bad joke, considering what happened at the Old Manse.

In case you don't know, Harvey and Greg visited the rich uncle last winter to request backing for a ski lodge, and Harvey was slapped down hard. College tuition—yes. Ski lodge—no. But Harvey didn't give up. He went to the Old Manse a second time—with a sketch pad and Clarissa. But when he mentioned the ski lodge property as an investment, Uncle Nathan vetoed it again. As the story goes, Harvey was so mad he refused to go to church when the whole household went on Sunday morning. What was he doing while the others were singing hymns?

I think—and Greg thinks—he was poisoning the air ducts. Greg says the black fungus can be scraped off old houses; it can be found under the wallpaper and in dark closets. He should know; his specialty is restoring old buildings.

At any rate, after their visit to the Old

Manse, Clarissa and Harvey broke up. She got a job at the *Something,* and Harvey's aunt and uncle became ill. "Allergies," they said. I'm very worried about them.

Does this sound like a synopsis for a crime story, Qwill? Or what?

Vicki

Qwilleran said, "My question is: What about Nathan's will?"

"Relax, Qwill. Nathan took care of that the day after Harvey was here last winter. He's leaving everything to the community. But I'll show this letter to the prosecutor. Harvey should be apprehended on suspicion of homicide."

Qwilleran thought, While the Ledfield household, including servants, was at church on Sunday morning, Harvey was implanting fungus in the air ducts of the master suite. . . . Koko knew from the beginning that Harvey was a murderer; that's why he dropped on his head—something he'd never done before.

. . .

By Tuesday morning Moose County was in an uproar! Two members of an important family had been murdered, and their nephew was being flown back from California as a suspect—under protective custody. Everyone was listening to WPKX newsbites; the grapevine was working overtime; the coffee shops were crowded; rumors were flying.

"He'll be lucky if he ain't lynched!"

"Wasn't he the son of that no-good brother?"

"Wanted their money. They had plenty."

"But they were never stingy."

"No kids of their own."

"Did you know he played the violin? His wife played the piano. They were pretty good, they say."

"How old were they?"

"Not too old. My sister used to see them in church."

"My next-door neighbor used to work for them. She said they were good people. Mrs. Ledfield even remembered my sister's birthday. Imagine that!"

"Too bad they never had kids."

"What will happen to their big house?"

"Somebody'll make a hotel out of it."

"Nah! Not in that neighborhood. Are you nuts?"

🐾 Qwilleran's phone rang incessantly but all calls were transferred to the answering machine, and he chose which to return—very few.

There was one he called back, Junior Goodwinter.

The young managing editor said, "How'd you like that for bad timing? No paper today! Just our Hurricane Special!"

"Could you throw together a Homicide Special?" Qwilleran suggested facetiously.

"You're not kidding. We'll do a memorial section on Thursday. Could you rustle up a *'Late Greats'* column? Any other suggestions will be appreciated."

"Maggie Sprenkle was their closest friend. She can tell you plenty—all in good taste."

"Would you call her? You seem to be her fairhaired boy."

Qwilleran huffed into his moustache. "What's the deadline?"

. . .

Moose County was mopping up. Although the storm had finished its dirty work, the sun was not exactly shining, and folks still wore the hurt expressions of citizens who had been punished for something they didn't do.

EIGHTEEN

🐾 Tuesday night WPKX kept the grapevine awake with hints about murder in high places.

Wednesday morning the *Something* published an extra, announcing the deaths of Nathan and Doris Ledfield, plus a bulletin that a Ledfield heir had been arrested in California. The entire edition sold out in two hours. And for the rest of the day, all telephone lines were busy throughout the county.

Qwilleran wrote so copiously in his private journal that he had to drive to the stationery shop for another notebook. Not the classic cloth-bound hardcover suitable for preservation in the Library of Congress. Not a slick black-and-chromium looseleaf. Just an ordinary school notebook with lined pages bound into an ugly brown plastic cover.

Behind the stationer, there was a print shop that had permission to reproduce Cool Koko's wise sayings on eight-by-ten cards suitable for framing, with proceeds going to animal welfare. (It's worth noting that a manufacturer of picture frames claimed to sell more eight-by-tens in Moose County than in the rest of the entire state.)

The most recent was: "Cool Koko says: Look before you leap on the kitchen stove."

From there Qwilleran went to the department store to buy a pair of socks he hardly needed.

Larry Lanspeak was busy in the front of the store. "Go back to the office," he said to Qwilleran. "Carol wants to see you."

Carol gave him a tearful greeting. "Oh Qwill! I can't believe the dreadful thing that happened! Liz Hart was killed on the Bloody Creek Bridge last night. Liz was like a second daughter to us!"

He commiserated the best he could and then

brought up the obvious question: "What will happen to the Old Grist Mill?"

"Her brothers will want to sell," Carol said, "and those sharpies in Lockmaster will want to buy, but we can't let them get a toehold in Moose County . . ." She paused and waited for a reaction. Getting none, she blurted, "Why don't you buy it, Qwill? . . . I mean, the K Fund?"

"Hmmm," he mused, aware of the feeling between the two counties. "The K Fund invests in local properties. You might suggest it to G. Allen Barter of HBB&A . . ."

"We know Bart very well!" Carol said with enthusiasm. "The Barters have a farm next to ours."

Qwilleran continued his walk through downtown, exchanging greetings with passersby— words and gestures that were more somber than usual.

On Main Street he automatically looked up at the second floor of the Sprenkle Building to see if the five "ladies" were in the five windows. This time one was missing. Was she unwell? Having a bite to eat? Or had she just excused herself? He stopped to watch, often wondering if the ladies could see him across the street, and if they would recognize his moustache. Then Maggie appeared in the window beckoning him urgently.

He crossed the street, waving thank you to the drivers who stopped to let him through the crowded traffic lanes.

At the entrance a buzzer admitted him, and he climbed the narrow stairs covered with plush carpet thick enough to turn an ankle.

As he expected, Maggie wanted to talk about the Ledfield tragedy.

Qwilleran said, "I regret sincerely that I never met the Ledfields."

"It would have been a case of mutual admiration," she cried. "Nathan admired your handling of the Klingenschoen fortune—and he always read the 'Qwill Pen' aloud to Doris. . . . Oh, Qwill!" She showed signs of another emotional outburst.

"Stay calm, Maggie. Remember and be thankful for all the years the Sprenkles and the Ledfields had together."

"I remember the beautiful hands of Doris and Nathan. Musicians' hands are long and slender. Doris said they exercised their fingers for fifteen minutes every day. Her fingers flew over the keys without seeming to touch them. And Jeremy used to marvel at Nathan's fingering of the violin strings. . . . I know you like music, Qwill. Would you like to borrow my collection of their piano and violin recordings? Polly has told me about your magnificent music system at the barn!"

She said, "My favorite is Chopin's *Polonaise Brillante*! You'll both love it!"

"I'd be honored," he said.

Then he added, "Friday's 'Qwill Pen' will be a '*Late Great*' profile of the Ledfields. Is there anything I should know?"

"I can tell you one thing," she replied with fervor. "They always did more than they were asked to do, and gave more than they were asked to give. They supported every worthwhile program: school, church, library, athletic, and civic."

Qwilleran said, "Did you know some of their mounted animals were in the *Pickax Then* parade?"

"Not only that, but his wildlife museum was open twice a year to schoolchildren who had the highest grades!" Maggie said.

"The Ledfields visited the barn once, paying three hundred dollars a ticket. It was a benefit for the local literacy program. I was not able to meet them due to an embarrassing incident with Koko that ended the evening early."

Maggie had to smile. "Doris told me it was the most fun they had had in years! Your cat stole the show."

"Koko disgraced himself, but the evening was a financial success for a good cause."

Maggie said, "Nathan called it the best fund-raiser he'd ever attended—and he'd gladly pay to see it again."

When Quilleran left he was carrying a leather case of recordings to play on the barn system. He stowed them in the trunk of his car.

Having declined Maggie's offer of "a nice cup of tea," he went instead to Lois's Luncheonette, where he could get a wicked cup of coffee and listen to the gossip. He called it "taking the public pulse."

He found the place in an uproar. Every chair at every table was filled. All the customers were talking at once—about the Ledfields—the murders . . . the family scandal— and the Ledfields' will. Especially the will! Who would inherit? How much? The possibility that the fortune might be going out of state. Everyone seemed to have a cousin or father-in-law whose wife knew the Ledfields' housekeeper or whose uncle was their window washer.

Qwilleran drank his coffee while standing at the cash register, then walked to the office of HBB&A, hoping Allen Barter would be at his desk. He was.

"What brings you out, Qwill?"

"I've been hearing strange rumors about the Ledfield bequests. Do I have to wait for tomorrow's newspaper?"

"Sit down and I'll fill you in. It's very simple. An old intermediate school will become the Ledfield Music Center, offering private lessons, classes, recitals, et cetera, all under the supervision of Uncle Louie MacLeod. . . . The Ledfield wildlife collection will be moved to a downtown site convenient for classes of schoolchildren. . . . The Old Manse will become a museum of art and antiques, with guided tours conducted by volunteers trained as guides, and with a respectable admission charge to discourage gawkers. Nathan envisioned it as an educational experience for visitors."

"Sounds good," Qwilleran said. "There are rumors that some of the fortune is going out of state."

"You've been hanging around the coffee shops, Qwill."

Next, Qwilleran left his car in the parking lot and walked to the newspaper. "Just touching base," he said to the managing editor.

"We'll be back to normal tomorrow," Junior said. "Will you have your usual 'Qwill Pen' for Friday?"

"I'll write a '*Late Great*' on the Ledfields."

"The terms of the will are scheduled to run tomorrow. It could be quite a sensation. The Ledfields go back to the nineteenth century, when mine owners made fortunes and there was no income tax. And they've had a century to invest it, so you know they were loaded. Whether they're leaving it to Moose County remains to be seen. . . . We're printing a large run tomorrow."

In the days that followed, Qwilleran's neighbors in the Village assumed he would stay there for the winter, since he had gone to the trouble of moving from the barn.

True, he had many friends there, and there were numerous activities in the clubhouse, but it could not compare with the barn for livability. The acoustics were magnificent, and he had a collection of the Ledfields' CDs waiting to be played. Altogether it was an odd situation. The barn made good country living in the city in the summer, and the condo made good city living in the country in winter.

Qwilleran pondered his options as he watched the cats gobble their dinner.

He asked, "Which shall it be, Koko? Stay here till spring . . . or move back to the barn now?"

Koko swallowed, made a few dental passes with his tongue and said "Yow-w-w" loud and clear!

And so, Qwilleran and the Siamese moved back to the barn—with its vast interior spaces, its balconies and ramps, its incredible acoustics.

Upon arrival, the cats first checked the bowls and plates (his and hers) under the kitchen table— then their private quarters on the third balcony. Yum Yum found her silver thimble. Koko remembered his new hobby: He dropped from a balcony railing, like a bombshell, into a cushiony sofa.

Pickax was glorying in its good fortune.

First, a former intermediate school was acquired for a music center, where young people could take piano or voice lessons from teachers commuting from Lockmaster. The high-school band could practice there without annoying the neighbors. Uncle Louis organized a choral club, and there was talk about staging a production of *The Mikado*.

Then an abandoned warehouse was adapted as a wildlife museum, and the Ledfields' mounted birds and beasts were exhibited in realistic settings created by the theatre club's set designer.

As for the Old Manse, it adapted well to a museum of art and antiques. Volunteers from the best families were trained as guides. There were fresh flowers in every room . . . the score of Chopin's *Polonaise Brillante* was open on Doris's Steinway grand and on Nathan's music rack (his Stradivarius was locked up).

A preview of the mansion was being planned for those willing to pay five hundred dollars for a ticket. Guides would conduct them.

Then—six months after the demise of Doris and Nathan, the Ledfield estate dropped a bombshell!

NINETEEN

After the doom and gloom of the hurricane, the accident at the Bloody Creek Bridge and—worst of all—the loss of the Ledfield family by unthinkable means . . . after all of this, Qwilleran and Polly were glad to be invited to the Rikers' condo for a Sunday afternoon repast.

"Less than a dinner," Mildred said, "but more than a lunch."

Qwilleran took Arch a bottle of something, and Polly took Mildred a silk chiffon scarf in a marbled pattern done by a local artist.

"The pattern is so unusual," Mildred cried. "And the silk is featherweight."

Polly said, "It's so weightless that I asked the druggist to put it on his pharmacy scale. He had to put a rubber band around it so it wouldn't float away. He said it weighed eleven and a half grams!"

Arch said, "If you roll it up it would fit in a shot glass!"

The first topic of discussion was the front-page story in Friday's paper: An anonymous donor had given the county-road commission a citizen's mandate to ensure the safety of the Bloody Creek Bridge according to the standard of the state engineers.

"Everyone," Arch said, "was wondering about the identity of the donor, but the release had come from a law agency, and secrecy was implied."

No conclusions were reached or even attempted. There was mumbled regret over the loss of Liz Hart . . . and consternation over the county's negligence.

Then the four survivors of the hurricane recalled their method of coping. Polly had phoned friends. Mildred had worked on the cookbook that's to be published. Everyone could guess how Arch had passed the time. As for Qwilleran, he always browsed through *Bartlett's Familiar Quotations* on a rainy day.

Now, to test the others, he asked, "Who is Gelett Burgess?"

In unison they responded, "I never saw a purple cow!"

"True! He had many talents but has been known for a century for a nonsensical poem. This past week I discovered a sequel to the original!"

He waited for their eager looks and then recited:

> *Ah, yes, I wrote the "Purple Cow"—*
> *I'm sorry, now, I wrote it!*
> *But I can tell you, anyhow,*
> *I'll kill you if you quote it.*

The others applauded.

Arch said he would rather be remembered for "The Purple Cow" than not remembered at all. And then Mildred said, "And we're all so proud to have the K Fund buying the Grist Mill! But who will replace Liz Hart? She was so charming!"

"Prepare for a surprise!" Qwilleran said. "A few years ago, when dining at the Boulder House Inn, did you occasionally meet a teenager? Her name was Jennifer."

They all remembered. She was very bright and personable. She was Silas Dingwall's daughter.

"Well, she has just completed a course in restaurant management at an eastern university. She and some fellow graduates have been traveling in France for gustatory experiences. She'll be perfect for the Grist Mill!"

"What a happy surprise!" Polly said.

Mildred added, "This has been a year of surprises, and I think there are more to come. I feel it in my bones!"

And so it went!

In September the Pickax Fourth of July parade took place on Labor Day.

In September, also, the Old Grist Mill opened under K Fund ownership—with a new manager.

In October, the Pickax Music Center opened

with the Andrew Lloyd Webber musical *CATS*, Uncle Louie MacLeod having secured the amateur rights to produce it. Besides, the choral group had all those costumes with tails left over from the *KitKat* review.

In October, also, Qwilleran moved his household back to the condo for the winter.

In November, the Ledfield Museum of Wildlife opened in a downtown warehouse, with mounted birds and beasts exhibited in naturalistic scenes created by the theatre club's set designers.

In December, a 500-dollar-a-ticket preview of the Ledfields' Old Manse raised $20,000 for child welfare. The sum was matched dollar-for-dollar by the K fund.

Also, in December, Koko became suddenly nervous—hearing inaudible noises and talking to himself. Qwilleran thought, something's going to happen! And then it happened!

In January, exactly six months after the demise of Nathan and Doris Ledfield, a sealed envelope that had long been in the vault of the law office was opened in the presence of witnesses. It was a document bequeathing a billion dollars for a Ledfield Academy of Music, specializing in keyboard and strings and of such excellence as to honor the name of Ledfield in music circles worldwide.

The announcement was released to news media from coast to coast. Included was an endowment in the form of blue-chip investments that would be available for expenses not covered by income from such an establishment.

There was one stipulation that stunned the witnesses and divided the good folk of Moose County. The magnanimous offer was made to any American city with a population of one million or more!

Press and pulpit lauded the Purple Point couple for their generosity in the past and their concern for the future quality of life in Moose County, specifically: the museum of art and antiques, a facility for the study and enjoyment of music, and a wildlife museum of interest.

Dissenters on the grapevine complained indignantly that the billion-dollar bequest should have stayed in Moose County to promote growth, build a new downtown, and improve recreation facilities.

What would Cool Koko say?

"When your dish is full of cream, don't expect more."

POSTSCRIPT
A NOTE FROM THE AUTHOR

Imagine my surprise, recently, when I received a phone call from James Mackintosh Qwilleran . . .

How nice to hear from you, I said. How's Koko? How's Yum Yum?

He said, *They're fine! Koko just put an idea in my head, staring at my forehead, the way he does, until something clicks. This time he suggested I should interview you for the "Qwill Pen" column, Lilian. Do you mind if I call you Lilian?*

Not as long as you spell it right.

The following dialogue took place:

First, I think my readers would like to know how long you've been writing.

My mother taught me to write at the age of three, but I was two years old when I composed my first poem: "Mother Goose is up in the sky and these are her feathers coming down in my eye."

Not bad for a beginner. When did you start writing fiction?

Nothing much until I was thirteen. I spent my summer vacation writing a French historical novel. All my favorite characters went to the guillotine and I cried a lot. My mother said I should write something that made me smile—and since mothers knew best in those days, I experimented with humorous verse. (Are you sure you want to hear all this, Qwill?) I invented the "spoem!"

Should I know what that is, Lilian?

They were verses about sports in what I called galloping iambic. One of my favorites was about a big-league player called McGee. Do you want to hear it? I know it by heart.

By all means! Wait until I turn on my recorder.

I think that I shall never see another gaffer in his prime who's stuck to baseball like McGee, untrammeled by the wear of time. Although McGee is getting gray, he never fails to fill the bill and slaps the horsehide twice a day, besides a frequent double kill, but when it comes to private tricks, McGee deserves the laurel bough; of all the superstitious hicks, it takes McGee to show them how!

He never has his turn at bat unless he walks around the ump and following an orange cat, he says, will cure a batting slump. His slumps indeed are very few; he says these tricks improve his skill, and if the fellow thinks they do it's 99 to 1 they will.

Bear in mind, Qwill, that I was seventeen when I wrote that. My interests changed. I wrote short stories, magazine features, advertising copy—and spoems. Then I started writing a newspaper column.

Apart from McGee's orange cats, Lilian, you haven't mentioned cats at all.

No, it was long after that when cats entered my life. I had always liked them, and they liked me. They followed me down streets in Paris, howled under my balcony in Rome, and sat on my lap, drooling, when I went visiting. It was not until I was living in a tenth-floor apartment that I was given a kitten. A Siamese. I called him Koko. But . . . It's difficult to describe what happened. Briefly: he was killed in a fall from the tenth floor. In a building full of cat lovers he was . . . murdered . . . by a cat hater. I was shattered! The only way I could get the tragedy off my mind was to write a short story about it. My story of murder and retribution was published in a magazine, and that is what led to the *Cat Who . . .* series.

Thank you, the "Qwill Pen" readers will appreciate it. May I ask you one more question, Lilian? Have you written plays? Your dialogue is smooth on the tongue and easy on the ear.

Thank you. I had an urge to write drama during the reign of Beckett, Albee, and Ionesco, but theatre of the absurd has passed its prime.

Bring it back! Pickax would be teeming with absurdities. Don't quote me.